SCROOGED

VI KEELAND
PENELOPE WARD

Cover designer: Sommer Stein, Perfect Pear Creative
www.perfectpearcreative.com
Proofreading by: Elaine York
Formatter: Elaine York, Allusion Graphics, LLC
www.allusiongraphics.com

SCROOGED

SEXYSCROOGE

CHAPTER 1

Meredith

"You've got to be kidding me," I mumbled to myself as I opened the front door to my apartment building. "Perfect. Just damn perfect." The wind howled and blew flakes the size of Frisbees into my face. I pulled up the hood of my coat, tucked a few wayward curls behind my ears, and tugged the strings to tighten it around my face. My eyes and nose were the only things that remained exposed. Squinting, I tried to see through the thick snowfall to look for my ride. A car turned onto my street, and the brake lights illuminated as he slowed and pulled to the curb. At least my Uber arrived quickly. At least I *hoped* it was my Uber, because I made a run for it without bothering to check the license plate.

My hood was still covering my face when I climbed into the back of the dark car and slammed the car door shut, which was probably why it took a few seconds to register the seat I'd just climbed into wasn't actually a seat.

"Umm. Excuse me," a deep voice said. The deep voice of—*a man whose lap I'd just climbed onto.*

1

Startled, things turned to shit after that.

I screamed directly into his face. Then proceeded to wind up and smack him straight across it.

"What the fuck?" the man yelled.

Clutching my chest, I felt my heart hammering against my rib cage. "Who are you? What the hell are you doing?"

"You just climbed into *my* Uber, jumped onto my lap, smacked me in the face, and you want to know *who I am*? *Who the hell are you*?"

"I thought it was *my* Uber."

The driver I hadn't even noticed decided to chime in. "This is a shared Uber. It's both your damn ride."

"Shared Uber?" Mr. Deep Voice said. "I didn't order any shared car."

He may not have, but I definitely *had* ordered from Uber Pool. It was cheaper, and God knows I needed to save a buck wherever I could. "I ordered a share."

It was then that I realized I was still sitting on the other passenger's lap. I lifted up my ass as best I could inside the confines of the back seat. "Umm. Do you think you can slide over so I'm not impregnated if we hit a bump?"

Mr. Deep Voice mumbled something I couldn't make out while sliding to the other side of the car. He dug his cell phone from his pocket and started to scroll. "I don't take shared cars. I'm sure this is some sort of mistake."

The driver huffed. "Well, you do today. Because that's what you ordered. It's either that, or you can get out and walk. Not too many other drivers are coming out in this mess today. What's it gonna be? My wife's got a ham cooking in the oven, and I got three-year-old twins who expect their gifts to be wrapped when they get up tomorrow morning. You're my last pick-up of the day."

Settling into my seat, I untied my hood and finally looked over at my fellow passenger. Figures he had to be gorgeous. With his thick glasses, square jaw, and broad shoulders, he reminded me of Clark Kent. Of course, I couldn't embarrass myself in front of an ugly guy. *God forbid.*

"Fine," the passenger grumbled. "Just go. I can't be late."

I leaned forward in my seat as the driver pulled from the curb. "Can you just make sure you drop me off first? I can't be late, either."

Clark Kent shook his head. "Sure. Jump on my lap, smack me, then make me late."

I'd totally forgotten that I'd hit him. "I'm sorry about smacking you. It was an impulsive reaction. But who sits inside a car on the curb side while waiting for another person to get in, anyway?"

"A person who thinks they aren't taking a shared Uber. I didn't even see you walking toward the car. It's a blizzard out there, in case you haven't noticed."

"Maybe next time you should be more careful when you order your Uber."

"There won't be a next time. Trust me."

"*Oh?* Did I scar you for life? You know *some men* might think it's their lucky day when a woman lands on their lap."

Clark looked up at me for the first time. His eyes did a quick sweep of my face. "I'm just having a shitty day. *Shitty month,* for that matter."

I was pretty sure that whatever shitty luck the gorgeous man next to me had as of late, it didn't hold a candle to my last few months. So, I decided to share. "Yesterday, I was on a bus that smelled like vomit. A sweet old lady took the seat next to me and proceeded to fall asleep with her head on my shoulder. When I got off the bus, I realized she'd pick pocketed me *and* stolen my watch. The day before that, a drunk guy in a Santa suit ringing a Salvation Army bell grabbed my ass when I walked by. I clocked him and then gave him a piece of my mind, only to turn around and find a Brownie troop had watched the entire thing—minus him grabbing my ass—and they all started crying. All they saw was that I'd punched Santa. Couple of days before that, I told my neighbor I'd watch her cat while she and her eight-year-old daughter went out of town for the night. I came home from work and the furry thing was laying in my bed, right where I sleep—*dead*. The little girl cries every time I see her in the hallway now. Pretty sure she thinks I'm a cat strangler. Oh...and let's not forget that today is Christmas Eve, and instead of heading to Rockefeller Center so that my boyfriend of four years can propose to me under the big tree—something I'd dreamed about since I was a little girl—I'm heading to court to get evicted by my money-hungry asshole of a landlord." I took a deep breath and let out hot air. "Shouldn't court be closed on Christmas Eve anyway?"

I'd apparently rendered him speechless with my tirade because he wasn't saying anything.

Clark Kent stared at me for a while before he finally said, "No, actually, courts never close on Christmas Eve, just Christmas Day. I've spent many Christmas Eves in court."

I arched my brow. "Oh yeah? You a criminal or something? Why is that?"

He cracked a smile. "I'm a trial attorney."

I squinted my eyes. "Really..."

"Does that surprise you?"

"Actually, no...come to think of it, you look like the stuck-up-suit type."

"Stuck-up suit?"

"Yeah, you know...pretentious, entitled, argumentative...know-it-all. That was my first impression of you, and the job fits."

"*Know-it-all*? Did you just call me smart?" He winked.

God, he's kind of adorable in an asshole-ish kind of way. Charming, too.

Maybe I should try being a little nicer.

CHAPTER 2

Rubbing my hands together, I stared out the window for a bit to gather my thoughts before turning to him again in an effort to be cordial. "So...where are you headed?"

"I have some quick business to take care of before I head home to Cincinnati for the holidays."

"To your wife and kids?"

He gave me a funny look through his glasses, like the answer to that was none of my business. "No, actually, I live here in New York. My parents are in Ohio."

"I see." I offered him my hand. "I'm Meredith."

He took it. "Adam." The warmth of his hand amidst this cold night felt better than a warm cup of Christmas cocoa.

"I'm sorry for unloading everything onto you like that." I blew a breath up into my blonde bangs. "I've had a major streak of bad luck lately."

He shook his head. "There's no such thing, beautiful."

His use of the word "beautiful" made me feel flush.

"What do you mean...no such thing?"

"No such thing as bad luck. You're in control of most things in your life, whether you know it or not."

Narrowing my eyes, I said, "How can you say that? No one is in control of everything."

"I said *most* things. The old lady who fell asleep with her head on your shoulder? You should've never let that happen. I mean, how can you have not known your watch was being removed? You should've been more vigilant. I will admit that Santa grabbing your ass and the cat dying weren't your fault. Shit happens. But the rent issue? That probably could've been avoided if you think back hard enough. I bet you're spending money you don't have, am I right? Money that could've gone toward rent. That Louis Vuitton purse had to have cost two grand. If you can't pay your rent, you shouldn't own a two-thousand-dollar bag."

I clutched my Louis Vuitton Pallas bag defensively, even though he was partially right.

This bag cost twenty-five hundred, to be exact, jerk.

How dare he tell me what I can and cannot own.

"You think you know everything? This was a gift from my boyfriend. I didn't buy it."

He smirked. "The one who's proposing at Rockefeller Center under the tree?"

I swallowed. "Well...*ex-boyfriend.* The one who will *not* be proposing to me under *any* tree. I'd had this stupid fantasy that he was going to ask me to marry him this year. We'd kiss under the tree at Rockefeller Center...and he'd bend me back in a dramatic dip."

He laughed. "That sounds like a scene out of a cliché, old movie—the dramatic dip. Not sure that happens in real life, beautiful."

Stop calling me beautiful, gorgeous.

"Yeah, well...none of that will be happening because he

dumped me for one of my friends, actually—right around Thanksgiving. I suppose that was my fault, too?"

His expression darkened. "Ouch. I'm sorry. No...not your fault. He's a douche. But it wasn't bad luck, either. Sounds like he did you a favor. I'd say that's *good* luck that you dodged a bullet."

I kind of liked that rationale. "You're right. I suppose that's a good way to look at it." I sighed and gazed out at the snow falling before I asked, "What about you? Do you have a significant other?"

Before he could answer, the car skidded on some ice. I instinctively grabbed onto Adam. To my mortification, I realized my hand wasn't on his leg. It was on his dick!

Whipping my hand off of him, I cringed. "Uh...I'm sorry."

My hand had lingered long enough to confirm that he was definitely packing.

"Apparently I have a magnet on my crotch, seeing as though it's not the first time this morning you *accidentally* made contact with my groin area."

Shit.

I cleared my throat. "That's right...it was an *accident*."

"Sure, it was." He chuckled then changed his tune when he got a load of my ashamed face. "I'm just kidding, Meredith. Jeez."

Something about hearing him utter my name in that deep voice did things to me.

Blowing out a breath, I tried to change the subject. "Anyway...you were saying..."

"I wasn't saying anything. You were being nosey and wanted to know if I had a girlfriend or a wife. Then, before I could answer, you grabbed my crotch."

I wouldn't even dignify that with a response.

"I'm single," he finally said.

My jaw dropped open. "Really? Why? You're attractive...successful...what's wrong with you?"

He bent his head back. "God, you sound like my mother."

I smiled. "Well, we both have a very good reason to wonder."

He looked contemplative, then shocked me when he said, "Actually, I was in a long-term relationship in my twenties, and she died of cancer. I haven't really wanted anything serious since. So..."

That left me speechless...absolutely gutted. How heartbreaking. "I'm so sorry."

He just stared at me for a bit. "Thank you."

"Goes to show...you never know what people have been through. I guess there are way worse things in life than getting kicked out of an apartment."

Adam nodded in understanding, and things fell quiet. The snow was falling so hard that you could barely see out of the windows.

I sighed. "I'm not sure either one of us is going to make it out of town tonight."

"Where did you say you're headed after court?" he asked.

"I didn't...say where I was going. But I'm scheduled to take a quick flight to Boston. My mother lives there. I'm spending Christmas with her."

"Will she be grilling you why you're still single, like mine does?"

"Umm...probably not."

"See. Your luck isn't so bad after all. Your mom will at least let you have a peaceful holiday."

I was a little embarrassed to admit the truth, but, hey, what's there to be embarrassed about after you've grabbed a man's junk? I turned to face Adam and swallowed my pride before speaking. "My mom won't be bugging me about being single because she thinks I'm still dating Tucker."

Adam quirked a brow. "Tucker? I figured he was a douche for dumping you after four years and dating your friend. But now I know he's a douche—one with a bad, frat-boy name." He chuckled. "*Tucker*. What the hell are you doing still pretending to date that tool anyway?"

I sighed. "I don't know. I haven't told anyone at work, either. Our framed picture is still on my desk. I guess at first I didn't want to say it out loud because it hurt too much. But now..." I looked down at my lap. "I'm not sure why I've kept it to myself. I suppose I'm embarrassed."

"Embarrassed? What the hell do you have to be embarrassed about? You didn't do anything wrong. You need to put that shit behind you. Get rid of doucheface's picture on your desk. You never know, there might be a whole slew of bachelors waiting for you to finally cut ties with that dick so they can ask you out."

I scoffed. "Yeah. I'm sure the line is out the door."

I felt Adam looking at me, but kept my eyes from meeting his. Eventually, he sighed. "Where do you work?"

"On 68th and Lexington, why?"

He looked at his watch. "Is your office closed today for Christmas Eve?"

"No. It's open. But not many people are in. Basically a skeleton crew. I took a vacation day."

Adam leaned forward and spoke to our driver. "Change of plans. Need to head back uptown and stop at 68th and Lex. We're making a quick stop. Keep the car running and wait for us, and I'll make it worth your while."

The driver looked in the rearview mirror. "A hundred dollars extra for the stop."

"A hundred bucks? Where's your Christmas spirit? I was thinking more like fifty."

The driver shook his head. "My kids sucked the Christmas spirit right out of me, along with the cash in my pockets. A hundred bucks. Am I turning around and Mr. Franklin is going to buy me a nice bottle of twelve-year-old Christmas spirit, or am I heading to drop you both off?"

Adam glanced over at me and our gazes caught. He considered his options while looking into my eyes, then spoke to the driver. "Fine. A hundred bucks. But I'm going to be late, so you need to step on it."

Our driver suddenly yanked the steering wheel to the left and the car started to fishtail. I grabbed onto the *oh-shit* bar above the door and held my breath until he regained control. The crazy man had just swung an illegal U-turn in the middle of New York traffic in a snowstorm. My heart was hammering inside my chest. "What the hell? Why is this lunatic taking us to my office?"

"Because you need help taking the first step. We're getting rid of the picture on your desk."

CHAPTER 3

"Is that...supposed to be a *moustache*?" Adam lifted his glasses for a better inspection of the photo of Tucker and me. We were standing in front of the dancing fountains at the Bellagio hotel in Vegas on Valentine's Day earlier this year. I'd thought he might propose on that trip. When he didn't, I convinced myself it was because he wanted to wait for Christmas so he could fulfill my childhood dream of a proposal and romantic kiss in front of the big tree. I was really fooling myself with him.

I sighed. "Tucker went through a phase after watching some Channing Tatum movie where he played a cop." Even though I saw the photo on my desk every day, it had been a long time since I really looked at it. His moustache was pretty bad. He'd shaved the bottom of it so that it was oddly positioned too high above his top lip. And it never fully filled in, so it was pretty ratty looking, too.

Adam opened the back of the frame and slipped out the photo. "Even if you liked the bad moustache, a dude trying to look like Channing Tatum should have clued you in that he was an idiot, beautiful."

I smiled. "I guess you're right."

He set the empty frame back on my desk and held up the photo. "Of course, I'm right. I'm always right. Now... would you like to do the honors, or should I?"

"I guess I should do it."

I took the photo from Adam's hand and stared at it for a moment. He really did look like an idiot with that moustache.

"Don't have all day. I'm already going to hear the judge lay into me for being late. Tear it up, sweetheart. It's like ripping a Band-Aid off of an old wound, just let it rip."

Taking a deep breath, I closed my eyes and tore the photo in two.

"That a girl. Keep going."

I smiled and ripped a second time. Then a third. It felt so good that I tore the damn thing up into tiny little pieces. When I was done, I dumped the shreds into the garbage can and looked up at Adam with an ear-to-ear smile on my face.

He smiled back. "You should do that more often."

"Rip up photos?"

Adam's eyes dropped to my lips. "No. Smile. You have a great smile."

My belly did a little somersault. "*Oh*. Thanks."

He cleared his throat and broke our gaze. "Come on, we better get going."

Outside, the snow was falling even heavier now. Adam grabbed my arm and we made a run for it, jumping back into our waiting Uber.

Once we were settled into the back seat, I said, "Thank you for that. I actually feel pretty good now. Which is a feat considering I'm heading to my imminent doom."

Adam unbuttoned the top of his coat. "What's the deal on your eviction anyway? You don't seem like the type to not pay your rent."

"I'm not. I paid my rent every month—early. But I don't really have the right to live there. The apartment I live in was my grandmother's. I moved in two years ago when she got sick so I could take care of her. It's rent-controlled. She died nine months ago. I love it there, so I stayed. I could never afford a one bedroom in my neighborhood. But the landlord recently found out and is having me evicted. He's also suing me for the market value of rent back to the date that my grandmother died since I didn't have a right to be there. He wants thirty-six-thousand-four-hundred-and-twelve dollars from me."

Adam looked at me for a long moment. "Thirty-six-thousand-four-hundred-and-twelve dollars, huh?" He scratched his chin. "Did you say you moved in two years ago and she died nine months ago?"

"Yeah. Well, I was rounding. Maybe I've lived there a few months less than two years. Why?"

"Did your attorney tell you about succession rights?"

"I don't have an attorney. I'm too broke. What are succession rights?"

"If you're related to a senior tenant and live with them for more than a year before they die, you can't be evicted and get to keep the rent control."

My eyes widened. "Are you serious?"

"Were you there a full year before she died?"

"I'm not sure! I moved in during the winter, and she died the following winter, but I don't remember the exact date I moved in."

"You'd need to prove it in court today at your eviction hearing."

My shoulders slumped. "How would I do that if I don't even know the date I moved?"

"You could try to estimate and let them know you need a little more time to gather the supporting documentation since you just became aware of your succession rights. Think about something you can use to back up the date, like moving expense receipts...anything. Depending on the judge, you might get a reprieve until after the holidays. They'll set another date, and you'll just have to prove the timeline."

Hope filled me, although I wasn't confident I had anything to show when I moved in.

"And if I can't prove it?" I asked.

"Don't worry about that. Deal with it when it comes."

"I already postponed once because I was sick. I don't think they're going to give me more time, no matter what I tell them."

"Maybe they'll want to go home early for Christmas, and you'll get lucky."

"Lucky, huh?" I teased. "I thought you said *luck* didn't exist?"

"Alright...you got me. Poor choice of words on my part. In this case you'd be presenting new information that would result in a possible extension. So, I still stand by what I said earlier. We create our own fate."

"Well, I maintain that my *luck* sucks lately, and I don't think that will change in court today. I'm not expecting a Christmas miracle."

"How you present yourself is everything, Meredith. If I've learned anything as an attorney, it's *that*. Now that you know what you may be entitled to, that throws a monkey wrench into the whole situation. If you make them believe you're confident in your estimation of when you moved in, I'd be willing to bet things will go in your favor."

His attitude was definitely motivating.

I tilted my head. "You really do believe that people can take their fate into their own hands, don't you?"

"A hundred percent. Mind over matter."

I paused, debating whether to ask my next question. "What can I do for *you?*"

He squinted. "What do you mean?"

"You've done some good things for me in such a short amount of time...helped me rip up that photo once and for all and made me aware of this loophole that could possibly save my behind. I owe you. Seriously...what can I do for *you,* Adam?"

He blinked a few times and didn't answer. I was starting to think that maybe that question sounded suggestive. Then something a little more PG than where my mind was going occurred to me.

I snapped my fingers. "Wait! I've got it."

He lifted his brow. "This doesn't involve you grabbing my crotch again, does it?"

See? He *had* taken my question the wrong way.

"No, wiseass."

He winked. "What is it?"

"You said your mother is always on your back about not having a girlfriend. Why don't you pretend you're dating me?"

"You gonna come home with me or something?" He chuckled. "I think I saw a movie like that once. A date dragged me to it."

"No. I won't be coming to Ohio. But we can take some photos and make it look like we're in a relationship."

He was amused. "You're suggesting that I do what you did with that photo of *Tucker?* Lie about being in a relationship?"

"Well, in this case, it would be harmless. You wouldn't be hanging onto an unhealthy memory...just fabricating a story to get your mom off your back for a bit. You could even say it's new, that we're just casually hanging out."

"You're asking me to lie to my mother..."

"Well...yeah, bu—"

"That's brilliant, actually." He scratched his scruff.

Relieved that he liked my idea, I grinned. "Yeah?"

"Yep. I may not even use it, but what the heck...I'll keep a photo on hand for an emergency if the nagging gets to be too much."

"Perfect!" I beamed. "Okay, grab your phone."

"Are you good at selfies?" he asked.

"Oh, yeah. I'm the selfie queen."

Over the next several minutes, I snapped a ton of photos of us together. The driver was looking at us through the rearview mirror like we were nuts.

I leaned my head into Adam's and smiled wide. In some of the shots, we stuck out our tongues, acted goofy. We truly looked like a happy couple who had been together for a while.

Adam smelled so incredibly good. He was wearing some kind of masculine musk that made my hormones rejoice. *Joy to the World!* I found myself not wanting to stop posing for photos just so I would have an excuse to smell him, be close to him.

At one point, he wrapped his arm around me, and chills ran down my spine as I felt the side of his hard body against mine.

God, Meredith. That's pathetic that you're resorting to cheap thrills now.

Clearing my throat, I reluctantly pulled away. "I think we have enough."

"You sure?" His eyes lingered on mine. Time seemed to stand still, and I got the sense that maybe he'd been enjoying the contact as much as I'd been. Or perhaps that was wishful thinking.

For a moment I became mesmerized by the reflection of the streetlights in his glasses as he continued to stare at me. Maybe I wasn't imagining the attraction. He *had* called me beautiful, complimented my smile. I'd assumed he was just pulling my chain, but maybe there *was* something there.

Anxiety started to build within me. This ride would be over soon. We'd be going our separate ways.

Would I ever see him again?

CHAPTER 4

I realized I was still holding his phone. "I'm just going to send myself a few of the photos," I said.

"Alright," he said as he watched me program my number into his contacts. I messaged myself the entire set of pictures we had taken. I suppose that was a great excuse to make sure I left him with my number.

After handing him back his phone, I asked, "Do you mind if I post one of these to Instagram?"

He hesitated, then said, "Go for it."

"I won't tag you or anything. Not that I even know your last name."

"Bullock."

Bullock.

Adam Bullock.

Meredith Bullock.

Adam and Meredith Bullock.

Mr. and Mrs. Adam Bullock.

The Bullocks.

I laughed inwardly at my ridiculous thoughts, as I stared down at our photo. "Do you want me to tag you?"

He shook his head. "I'm not on Instagram."

"Are you too cool for social media?" I teased.

"I went on there to see what the hype was all about once and accidentally liked someone's photo from five years ago. Figured that made me look like a creep, so I vowed never to go on there again."

I was cracking up. "I hate when that happens."

After uploading my favorite photo of us—one where his arm was around me, I applied the Gingham filter and the hashtags: #AnUberChristmas #NewFriend #DontKnowHimFromAdam #ClarkKent

"Let me see," he said, taking the phone from me. He stared at the photo and rolled his eyes. "Clark Kent, huh?"

"You remind me of him...in a good way."

"My muscles?"

I giggled. "Your glasses. But now that you mention it... your muscles, too." I felt my cheeks heat up after offering him that compliment.

Adam began to scroll through my other photos, most of which were of food. "Now, I see where most of your money goes. You're a foodie."

"Yes. I love taking elaborate photos of my meals in various lighting."

"You're very artistic."

I couldn't tell if he was bullshitting me. "Thank you."

When he handed me back my phone, his hand landed on mine for a few seconds.

As much as I'd hoped to see him again, I honestly couldn't fully read him. He'd alluded to the fact that he chose to remain single after losing his girlfriend to cancer in his twenties. Did that mean he wanted to be single forever?

How old is he anyway?

"How old are you?"

"Thirty-one," he answered. "You?"

"Twenty-eight." I smiled. "'Bout time I got my shit together, right?"

"Nah. You're good. You don't need to do anything differently."

I shrugged. "I would hardly say that."

"You're a bright, attractive woman who stopped her life to take care of her sick grandmother. You're just getting back on your feet between that and your douchnozzle ex throwing you that curveball."

Once again, his words had soothed my soul somehow. Maybe I needed to take a bit of Adam's advice, take my fate into my own hands. I got the sudden urge to ask him if he'd want to hang out sometime in the New Year. Maybe he was the type of guy who needed a clear signal, especially if he was closed off when it came to women.

My heart started to beat faster as I readied to pose my bold question.

Before the words had a chance to escape my mouth, the car skidded on some ice, sending us into a snow bank.

This time, Adam had come crashing into my direction. I felt his large hand on my knee.

"Are you okay?" he asked before promptly removing it.

No, put it back.

"Yeah," I said as my heart pounded from the adrenaline rush.

The car wasn't moving. The tires were rolling but we weren't getting any traction. We were now stuck in the snow.

Crap! I was going to be late for my hearing.

The driver finally said, "You guys better go. I think I'm gonna be here for a while. The courthouse is only a couple of blocks that way. You can walk."

I looked at the time on my phone and turned to Adam. "I'm actually running late. I have to go." I waited a bit for him to say something, to give him a chance to make a move, but he just looked at me.

After I reluctantly exited the car, I realized he was getting out, too, and coming around to where I was standing on the sidewalk.

"Let's go," he said.

I perked up. "You're coming with me?"

"Yeah. I'm going to the courthouse, too. That was always the plan."

I hadn't realized that, even though it made sense, given that he was an attorney.

"Oh, for some reason, I didn't think we were going to the same exact place."

As we trudged through the snow together, I no longer felt brave enough to ask him out. That car mishap had apparently knocked the courage right out of me, or maybe knocked some sense into me.

When we arrived at the entrance, I had to wait in a long line, while Adam could breeze right through the *attorney only* door. I held out a last bit of hope that maybe he'd ask to see me again, but was disappointed when he merely gave me a wave.

"Good luck today, Meredith. Whatever you do, just be extra nice to the plaintiff's attorney, and I'm sure you'll get what you need."

I half-heartedly smiled. "Thanks. It was nice meeting you, Clark Kent."

He walked through the metal detectors and yelled back to me in line. "You, too, beautiful."

"All rise. The Civil Court of the City of New York is now in session, the Honorable Daniel Ebenezer presiding. Everyone please remain standing until the judge has entered and is seated."

Daniel Ebenezer? *Really*? I couldn't make this shit up if I tried. I was about to be tossed out on my ass by *Scrooge* on Christmas Eve? I started to laugh because it was so absurd. The bailiff shot me a warning glare, so I managed to turn my laughter into a cough until I settled down.

A judge in a black robe took his seat and everyone in the courtroom followed his lead. He put on reading glasses and buried his nose in some papers, then looked over at the bailiff. "Well, what are you waiting for? Let's get started. Call the first damn case."

Great. Just great. He really *was* Scrooge.

The bailiff cleared his throat. "Schmidt Real Estate Holdings vs. Eden. Docket number 1468944R."

Wow. I'm first.

Nerves hit me full force as I stood and approached the little gate that separated the players from the audience. The bailiff nodded for me to enter and pointed to the right side of the courtroom where there was a lonely looking empty table.

A minute later, the squeaky little gate opened and closed again, and a suit walked over to the table on the other side of the court. I was so nervous that I hadn't even looked over to check out my adversary...until I heard his voice.

"Your honor. Adam Bullock representing Schmidt Real Estate Holdings. We've been in discussions with the plaintiff and request an adjournment."

My head whipped to Adam. *Adam* was my nemesis? And what was he doing requesting an adjournment?

The judge inched his glasses down his nose and spoke over them. "This case has already been adjourned once, Counselor. My docket is not your playground. Why can't this be heard or settled today?"

Adam looked over at me. "Your honor, Miss Eden has provided some evidence that she may be entitled to succession rights. We'd like a little time to authenticate that evidence."

The judge glanced over at me. "I take it you're fine with this adjournment, Miss Eden?"

I was so stunned that I could barely speak. "Umm. Yes. Yes, Your Honor. Yes, I am. That would be great."

The judge scribbled something down and spoke without looking up. "Re-calendared for Tuesday, February 14th, and I expect this to be worked out on that date." He banged his gavel, and I stood there in shock.

I'm not evicted?

It's over?

Oh my God.

My mouth hung open. I continued to stand there and just stare into space.

Adam walked over and extended a paper my way. His voice was all business. "You'll need to fill this out, Miss Eden."

I didn't know what to say, so I just took the paper from his hand. "Oh. Okay. Thank you."

Adam lifted his chin to the bailiff, and, without another glance my way, he was gone. By the time I finally lifted my jaw off the floor, he was already walking through the courtroom door into the lobby.

I picked up my purse and shook my head in disbelief. Outside of the courtroom, I looked around. Adam was nowhere in sight. This was the craziest day ever. I waited a few minutes to see if he'd come back to talk to me, but he didn't. So, eventually I headed to the ladies' room, and figured I'd call an Uber once I was done.

But when I went into the bathroom, I started to fold up the paper in my hand—the paper I'd completely forgotten that Adam had handed me—and noticed that there was something written in pen on it.

Meet me outside. I'll get the Uber.

My heart started to pound. *Oh my God.* Forgetting I needed to pee, I took off for the front door of the courthouse. Through the whiteout conditions of the snow, I saw Adam getting into a Town Car. I didn't bother to waste time with my jacket or hood; I just made a run for it—slipping and sliding all the way, barely avoiding falling twice to get to the curb.

Adam opened the car door with a giant smile and laughed. "Get in here. You're going to break something."

I was out of breath and on a high when I slammed the car door shut. "I can't believe it was you!"

"Guess there is a such thing as luck after all."

"I...I have no idea how to thank you."

He winked. "That's okay. I have a few ideas."

The car slowed to a stop. Adam wouldn't tell me where we were going, but we definitely weren't heading to the airport or back to my apartment. But, I didn't care. I never wanted to get out of this Uber. Not only was I sitting next to a hot guy who smelled good, but he'd saved my ass from being homeless on Christmas Eve—from Ebenezer Scrooge, of all people. I had no doubt that the judge would have evicted me had things not worked out the way it did.

Adam opened the door, and I looked up at where we were. "Rockefeller Center?"

"You said you loved the tree. Figured our flights were probably delayed anyway." He shrugged. "And if we miss them...that wouldn't be such a bad thing either, would it?"

I beamed from ear to ear. "No, it definitely wouldn't be."

Adam exited the Town Car and held out his hand to help me out. He didn't let go even after the Uber started to pull away. His hand was warm and so much bigger than my little one. We walked side by side to the tree. I really did love it here. Rockefeller Center at Christmas was a magical place, even if I didn't get my proposal.

Adam and I stood and stared up at the tree. He looked at me and then stopped a couple walking by. "Excuse me. Would you mind taking a picture of us in front of the tree?"

They both smiled. "No, not at all."

Adam fiddled with his cell and handed it to the woman.

"You ready, beautiful?"

I'd assumed he meant to smile big for the camera. So I did.

But obviously he had something else in mind. He grabbed me into his arms. "Meredith Grab-my-junk Eden, you stole my Uber, snapped photos so I can lie to my mother, and made me commit perjury to a judge today, and yet I haven't smiled this much on Christmas Eve in years. Will you do me the honor of putting this picture in the empty frame on your desk?"

I laughed. "I'd love to."

With a big smile on both our faces, Adam bent me backwards into a deep dip, and planted his lips over mine.

It just goes to show that with a little luck, fairy tales can come true, despite Ebenezer Scrooge.

THE END

Merry Christmas and Happy Holidays!
Much Love,
Vi & Penelope

THE MERRY MISTAKE

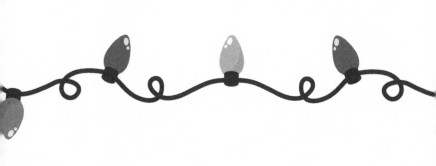

CHAPTER 1

Piper

It was a lazy Saturday on the Upper West Side. Christmastime in New York was always my favorite time of the year. From the hustle and bustle of passersby with their shopping bags, to the lush wreaths on the doors of the brownstones in my neighborhood, I just loved every bit of this season. The air was so cold today that it felt like a true cleanse of my system every time I breathed it in.

I'd just left one of my favorite cafés, where I'd spent the afternoon sipping hot cocoa and looking through some catalogs to get ideas for an apartment I was re-doing. As an interior designer, browsing for décor was one of my favorite things to do, even in my spare time when I wasn't on the clock; I really didn't even consider it a chore.

As I approached my apartment building, I noticed a man sitting down on the ground right in front of it. From time to time, the homeless would choose a spot outside of my building, probably figuring that it was a nice, safe area. Unfortunately, all too often, residents would complain, forcing those poor people to move. I never had an issue with the homeless parking themselves outside our building. It wasn't like they were hurting anyone.

Rather than approach this man, I had an idea. Turning back around, headed in the direction from which I came, I walked toward my favorite delicatessen. My plan was to buy the man a damn good lunch and give him some cash. After all, that gesture would be right in line with my decision this year to forego Christmas gifts to my friends and family in favor of good deeds. Rather than spending money needlessly on a scarf or Broadway show tickets, I'd help someone in need and let each friend and family member know exactly what I'd done for someone else in their honor. So, who was going to be the lucky recipient of today's good deed? I figured helping this homeless man, buying him lunch, and giving him some cash might be the perfect present for my Aunt Lorraine.

When it was my turn in line at the deli, I said, "Large pastrami on rye, please." After placing my order, I grabbed a bottle of Coke from the refrigerator, a bag of sour cream and onion chips, and a large chocolate chip cookie from the counter that was covered in Saran wrap. Not knowing what the man liked, I basically just ordered all of my own favorites. You couldn't go wrong with anything from this place.

Returning to the sidewalk and feeling good about myself, I headed back toward my building. I'd also slipped a fifty-dollar bill into the paper bag.

Luckily, the man was still sitting in that same spot on the ground when I returned. From a distance, I could see he was wearing a flannel shirt. Or was it a jacket? As I approached, I also noticed ripped jeans. A baseball cap covered his face.

Now standing right in front of the man, I bent down and cleared my throat. "Hello...I'm Piper. I, uh, thought you might be hungry," I said, reaching the bag out to him.

He didn't immediately say anything as he lifted his hat a bit so he could see my face through the sun. Even though it was a cold day, the sun was shining brightly.

I added, "There's also a fifty-dollar bill inside the bag. All I ask is that you don't spend it on alcohol."

He opened the bag and took a whiff, then said, "Then it's okay to spend it on strippers?"

Not knowing how to answer that, I stammered," Uh...I'd prefer you didn't, but whatever makes your Christmas merry, I suppose."

He abruptly lifted his hat off his head. That was when I noticed his striking blue eyes, head full of thick, beautifully tousled copper hair, and really handsome face.

His eyes seared into mine as he said, "What are you smoking, lady?"

I swallowed. "What do you mean?"

"You think I'm *homeless*?"

Oh.

No

What?

He's not homeless?

In an attempt to defend myself, I cringed and said, "Why else would you be sitting on the ground outside of this building?"

"Oh, I don't know...maybe I'm doing some work inside and came out for a smoke?" He scowled. "Any number of things."

It was then that I really took a moment to look at him. He wore one of those heavy flannel shirts that were more padded like a jacket, the ones I'd always see construction workers donning. *Of course.* From a distance, he somehow looked like he might be homeless, but up close he looked like something out of an L.L. Bean catalog. He wasn't just handsome; he was gorgeous. He had the perfect amount of chin scruff and large hands that looked like they'd seen their share of work. He looked...sexy. Not homeless. Not homeless at all, *you idiot, Piper.*

With every second that passed, I started to realize just how much of a mistake I'd made. The rips in his jeans were intentional, not a result of tattered wear. He was clean and didn't look anything like someone who lived on the streets with limited access to a shower. Rather than smelling bad, he smelled quite good in fact, like cologne with a hint of cigarettes.

"Clearly, I made a mistake. But you were sitting on the ground...I jus—"

"So, if someone takes a rest on the ground, they're automatically homeless?"

"We've had homeless people camp out in this very spot before, so it seemed plausible."

He scratched his chin. "Let me ask you this, Piper...if a hooker walks the streets in heels, bending down talking to strangers, does that mean that every woman walking the sidewalk in heels—such as yourself—who bends down and talks to strangers is a hooker?"

Is he indirectly calling me a whore?

Plain and simple, I'd tried to do a good thing. And I fucked up. But that was no reason for him to be so mean.

"Look, I'm sorry. Clearly this was a huge misunderstanding. I was just trying to do something good for someone."

"So you could feel better about yourself..."

I squinted. "Excuse me?"

"By labeling someone you perceive as beneath you, it makes you feel better about yourself. Further solidifying the entitled rich girl that you are."

No, he didn't.

Despite the frigid air, my body temperature started to rise.

"I'll have you know, I work very hard for my money. There's not a spoiled or ungrateful bone in my body."

"Perhaps, then, you should do your research before handing your cash out to random people on the sidewalk. But it didn't matter to you. You didn't care who you were handing it to, as long as you were getting your fix of self-righteousness."

This prick was getting on my last nerve.

"I don't know who you are, or what you're even doing outside of my building, but—"

"Finally...she asks who I am!" He stood up. "Might that have been a good idea *before* you handed me fifty dollars and a bag of food?"

"You know what? I am sort of wishing now that it were a bag of *dicks* instead, because that's what you deserve...to eat a bag of dicks!" I huffed, "I'm done with this conversation. Have a nice day. Stuff the sandwich up your ass and use the money to buy yourself some manners!"

It had taken me hours to calm down from that infuriating encounter.

Later that evening, I was headed out with a friend when I stopped at the sight of something at my feet just outside my apartment door.

It was a paper bag. Upon closer inspection, it looked like the same paper bag I'd given to that guy earlier—because it said Rick's Delicatessen on the front.

Hesitantly, I picked it up and opened it.

I gasped at the sight of what looked like seven rubber dildos inside in various colors.

What the fuck?

There was a note.

*Per your suggestion, I went ahead and bought a bag of dicks. Actually, technically, you said you wished you'd given me a bag of dicks and that I should buy some manners, but they don't sell manners on 8th Avenue. As luck would have it, they **do** sell dicks. So, wish granted. While I'm unable to "eat" them as you so kindly suggested...(because, you know, you're such a nice, giving person who cares about your fellow man), I figured you might get more use out of a bag of dicks than me. Merry Christmas and Happy Holidays!*

P.S. The food and the fifty you left me with went to an *actual* homeless person as per your intention.

CHAPTER 2

Piper

I smiled looking in the mirror.

It had been a long time since I looked at my reflection and saw someone I liked.

This emerald green cocktail dress had been in the back of my closet with the tags on it for the better part of two years. Last week I'd gone to *Second Chances*, a luxury resale consignment shop here in the city, to sell the last of my designer purses. Since they bought anything name brand, I brought along some of my gently worn designer clothes and also this fancy, never-worn dress. I couldn't remember how much Warren had paid for it, but then again, I didn't look at price tags back then, not even when we shopped at Barneys where we'd bought it. But when the consignment store offered me a whopping thirty dollars for a Limited Edition Valentino, I'd decided to keep it. I could wear it once and sell it on eBay for ten times what they were willing to pay. This dress was not leaving my hands for less than a few hundred dollars, even if I could use the money to put toward next month's rent.

Tonight I was going to my friend Avril's annual Christmas party. I'd been looking forward to it for weeks. Since I was broke, I didn't get to see my friends too often. My days of paying eighteen dollars for a glass of wine in a Manhattan bar were over. Avril would undoubtedly have three-hundred-dollar-a-bottle champagne and Beluga caviar, and I was honestly looking forward to a little indulgence.

I lined my lips in blood red and grabbed a wool cape from the closet. But then on second thought, I traded the pretty cape for a heavy parka. It was freezing out, and since I wasn't about to pay for an Uber, I could be standing at the bus stop for a while. Side note...when I often told people how much happier I'd been since I started shedding the 'extras' in my life, I hadn't been referring to Uber. I missed Uber something fierce.

I took the elevator down to the lobby and stepped off ready to take Manhattan on.

"*Wheet-whoo.*" A whistle from behind me turned my head. I found my elderly neighbor sitting in his wheelchair.

"Mr. Hanks? What are you doing down here?" My brows drew together. "And in your pajamas?"

"Waiting for pretty girls. I guess I can go back up now."

I laughed. "Well, thank you. I'm heading to a Christmas party. Do you need some help before I go?"

"Nah. You go on and have a good evening."

"You, too, Mr. Hanks."

I walked through the lobby and exited the door. My phone buzzed as I hit the cold air, so I paused to dig it out of my coat pocket and tugged off my gloves to text.

Avril: Why aren't you here yet?

Piper: Ummm... because it's only seven o'clock.

Avril: The party starts at seven.

Piper: Yes, but who comes on time?

Avril: Finn Parker...that's who.

Oh wow. I hadn't even realized he would be there. I'd met Finn last year, and we'd really hit it off. He'd given me his number, though I'd never called. It had been only a few days before my surgery, and I'd been in a dark place after I got out of the hospital...definitely not ready to jump into anything new—no matter how deep his dimples were. Plus, I'd just broken things off with Warren, and dating was the last thing on my to-do list. Though, now...it had been a *long year* of celibacy. I typed back.

Piper: On my way!

Avril: Hurry. He said he can only stay for an hour or two.

As I yanked my gloves back on, I turned around to look into the lobby. Mr. Hanks was still sitting there in his wheelchair. I looked at my phone again, then at the elderly man in the lobby, then my phone. Sighing, I tucked my cell into my pocket and opened the door to go back inside.

"Mr. Hanks. Is everything okay?"

He put on a smile that didn't quite reach his eyes. "Sure. Everything's just fine."

I noticed a yardstick a few feet away from his chair.

Narrowing my eyes, I asked. "Did you...drop that stick?"

Mr. Hanks frowned. "Oh, yeah. I guess I must've."

I picked it up and handed it to him. Two months ago, Mr. Hanks suffered a pretty bad stroke. It left him with limited mobility in both his arms, and one weak leg. I thought the stick might've been the only way he could reach the elevator button. I'd been so worried about getting to my party, that I hadn't even stopped to think that maybe he wasn't choosing to sit in the lobby with his mail on his lap. God, I was an idiot...leaving a nice neighbor in his pajamas in the lobby to run off to a party.

I pushed the button on the wall. "I actually forgot something, so I'm going back up to our floor," I lied. "Why don't we ride up together?"

The elevator arrived, and I got behind Mr. Hanks's electric wheelchair and pushed, even though there was a little remote on the arm of it he could've used. "So what are you doing for the holidays this year? Any big plans?"

"My son wants me to come to his place. He says he's cooking, but I got my money on that he takes the stickers off the food trays before I get there so I won't know he catered Christmas. My wife Mary Jean always made a big meal on the holidays...fish on Christmas Eve and a ham and lasagna on Christmas day. She tried teaching the kid how to cook, but he was always too busy conquering the world when he got older. Mason's a good kid, don't get me wrong, but he works too much."

I frowned. "My mom used to make lasagna, too. And fresh baked bread and pumpkin pie. Some kids loved waking up on Christmas morning to see what Santa brought. I loved waking up to a house that smelled like pie."

The elevator doors dinged on our floor, so I pushed the wheelchair out and down to Mr. Hanks's apartment. We lived on opposite sides of the elevator. When I arrived at his door, it was already open.

"Did you leave it this way?"

"Yeah. I can push it open with my foot, but getting the key in can still be a bit tricky."

"Oh. Yeah. I would imagine."

I wheeled Mr. Hanks inside and stopped at the kitchen doorway. The room was a disaster. It looked like robbers had ransacked the place. Two cans were on the floor, along with a few utensils, a roll of duct tape, cookies, and a gallon of milk that had spilled into a giant white puddle on the floor. And the kitchen sink water was running. I sidestepped the spill and twisted the faucet off. Glancing around at the mess again, I frowned at the two soup cans on the floor.

"Mr. Hanks, did you...eat dinner tonight?"

"Yeah, sure. I'm just a little messy. Ignore it in here. The aide that my son makes hang around here all day made dinner before she left. I'm just living the life of a bachelor."

Something told me he was lying. "What did you eat for dinner?"

"Soup."

I bent and picked up the empty plastic milk container and then walked over to the garbage. Using my foot to press the pedal to open the lid, I took a look inside before tossing the container in. *No soup can.* Mr. Hanks was a proud man. One who would rather sit in the cold lobby than ask me to pick up a stick so he could reach the elevator button.

"Mmm. I haven't had soup in a long time. Would you... mind if I had some?"

He squinted at me, but I smiled and he seemed to forget his suspicions. "Sure. Help yourself, kiddo."

I went back behind his wheelchair and brought him into the living room. Picking up the remote, which was also on the floor, I placed it into his hand. "Why don't you relax, and I'll I check out what my soup choices are, if you don't mind."

He nodded. "Help yourself."

Back in the kitchen, I took off my coat, collected the paraphernalia from the floor, and cleaned up the spilled milk. When I finished, I took out a pot and yelled to Mr. Hanks. "I can't decide between chicken dumpling and beef barley. They both sound so good. What do you recommend?"

He yelled back. "The beef barley is all barley and not enough beef, if you ask me."

Chicken dumpling it is.

While I heated two cans of soup, I finished straightening things in the kitchen and then set the table for two in the dining room. I buttered some white bread, like my mom used to do whenever she made me soup, and walked back to his chair.

"I hope you don't mind joining me. I hate to eat alone."

"Sure. Of course."

I set him up at the table and then watched while he struggled. His hand was so shaky that the soup would splash off the spoon before he could bring it to his mouth.

"Would it be okay if...I helped you with that?"

His shoulders drooped, but he nodded.

We talked while I fed him.

"I haven't seen that boyfriend of yours around in a while."

"Warren? We split up about nine months ago."

"Was that your doing?"

I nodded. "Yeah, it was."

"Good. His shoes were too damn shiny."

I laughed. "And that's a bad thing? Having shiny shoes?"

"Don't get me wrong. I liked to clean up for my Mary Jean every now and again, and that meant busting out the polish until I could see my ugly face in a wingtip. But the shoes on that man of yours sparkled every damn day. It ain't normal for a man to not have a few scuff marks every once in a while."

Warren definitely cared too much about his appearance. I'd never noticed, but I guess that did run from the top of his impeccably groomed hair to the shine of his shoes. I smiled. "He also used more hair products than me."

Mr. Hanks shook his head. "These men today, they're too soft. Is that why you dumped Shiny Shoes? He took longer than you to get all dolled up?"

I thought about making up something, like I did for almost everyone who asked what happened to my four-year relationship, but then I decided to be honest. "I went through a rough time, and he wasn't really there for me. So I told him I needed a break to deal with some personal stuff I was going through. For the last year of our relationship, I'd suspected that he might be having an affair with his assistant. Two weeks after I asked for the break, I ran into him unexpectedly on the street. He was holding hands with his assistant. Needless to say, our break turned into a permanent separation."

Mr. Hanks looked at me funny. "You suspected he was stepping out on you for *a year* and never said anything?"

I sighed. "Yeah. It's funny, after the thing ended, I asked myself why I never called him out on it. I think the truth was, I didn't really want the answer because down deep I knew it already. To be honest, neither of us loved each other the way we should've to spend four years together."

"So why didn't you kick him to the curb sooner?"

I spooned Mr. Hanks the last bit of noodles from the soup and sighed. "I think I just had my priorities wrong. Warren comes from a nice family. He's well educated and was very generous to me. My life with him would have just been... easy."

"My wife used to have a saying, *what comes easy won't last.*"

I smiled. "Your wife sounded like a smart lady." Mr. Hanks hadn't even noticed that I'd fed him both his full bowl of soup and mine. I stood with the empty bowls in my hand and winked. "And something tells me that she was talking about *you* when she repeated that saying."

I wound up hanging out with Mr. Hanks for three more hours. He told me story after story about *his* Mary Jean. Clearly she'd been the love of his life, and the five years since her death hadn't dulled how much he missed her. Avril had lit my cell on fire texting to ask where I was, and she wasn't happy when I responded hours later that I'd decided not to come because I developed a headache. But it was easier to tell a little white lie than to explain I'd been enjoying hanging out with my eighty-year-old neighbor more than I thought I'd enjoy her party.

When Mr. Hanks yawned, I took that as a signal that it was time to go. I grabbed my coat. "Would you like me to wheel you into the bedroom?"

He shook his head. "I'm a little rusty, but if you're trying to make a pass at me, I'm afraid you're a little too young."

I laughed. "You sure, you're okay?"

"I am." He smiled. "I'm good, sweetheart. And thanks for tonight. Especially the soup."

⁂

I ended up checking in on Mr. Hanks at least once a day after that. We'd become good friends fast.

And now it was Christmas Eve. I planned to stop over and see him with a pie I'd baked from one of my mom's old recipes. I'd hang out with him for a bit and then leave to head to a family party in New Jersey.

With my pumpkin pie in hand, I knocked on Mr. Hanks's door. Expecting that he was probably wheeling himself to greet me on the other side, I had a big smile on my face in anticipation of the reaction he'd have when he saw me standing here with this delicious-smelling pie.

But when the door opened, it wasn't Mr. Hanks who answered. It was...*him*.

Him!

The gorgeous, not-homeless man who'd given me the bag of dicks. Except tonight he wasn't dressed in a flannel work shirt and ripped jeans. He wore a blue fitted dress shirt and black trousers. He smelled like musky heaven, too.

He grinned mischievously. "You..."

"You," I repeated, then looked beyond his broad shoulders. "Where is Mr. Hanks?"

"He's just in the bathroom."

"What are you doing here?" I asked.

Before the guy could answer me, we were interrupted by the sight of Mr. Hanks cruising toward us.

He smiled. "I see you've met my son, Mason!"

CHAPTER 3

Mason

I still had no idea what she was doing in my father's apartment with a pie. *They apparently know each other?*

"This is my good friend, Piper," he said.

"Good friend? You never mentioned her to me."

"Sure I did! She's the one who comes over and has soup with me."

I nodded. "Ah, alright. You never said her name."

Dad smirked. "You weren't expecting her to be such a looker? Your old man can hang with the best of 'em, you know."

Piper blushed and set her pie down on the counter. She looked absolutely gorgeous in a dress that was the color of cinnamon. Piper looked even more beautiful than the several times I'd fantasized about her since our first meeting. Each and every fantasy would end with us angry fucking. I never thought I'd actually see her again. I knew she lived here, but everyone generally kept to themselves.

My father wheeled himself over to the counter. "You brought your mom's pumpkin pie."

46

"You remembered." She smiled. "It sure is."

He rubbed his stomach. "I can't wait to try it."

It was like my elderly father had been living a double life that included hanging out with hot women who brought him food. *And here I was feeling bad for him most days.*

She flashed me a taunting look. "Mason and I have actually met before, Mr. Hanks."

Shit. Here we go.

Dad turned to me. "No kidding? When?"

My body went rigid, and I said nothing as I braced for her explanation. I hoped she didn't throw me under the bus and tell my father what an ass I acted like that day.

"Yeah. He was outside the building one afternoon. We got to talking, didn't we, Mason?"

"Yes, we did." I grinned. "Piper actually shared her lunch with me. Is that how the story went?"

"Something like that. You were extremely charming from what I remember."

"I remember you being *charming* as well," I teased.

She turned to Dad. "And to thank me for sharing lunch with him, your son left me a nice thank you gift at my apartment door later that day—which, by the way, I've gotten a ton of use out of." Piper winked.

Fuck. Me.

She didn't just say that.

My pants suddenly felt tighter.

I cleared my throat. "Good to know. I figured you might need something like that. You seemed a little wound up."

"Indeed, I was that day." She looked down at my father. "You've raised an amazingly polite and thoughtful son, Mr. Hanks. You should be very proud."

My dad chuckled. "Well, whattya know. And here I was thinking he was a bit of a dick."

Piper burst into laughter, and I followed suit. Her eyes twinkled with mischief. I was grateful that she hadn't ratted me out. Truthfully, I'd regretted my knee-jerk reaction that day. The little gift I'd left her was my attempt at an apology, although it might not have come across that way. It pleased me that she was joking about it.

"Are you spending Christmas Eve here with your dad?" she asked.

"Yeah. It's just the two of us, and he refuses to come to my place. So, I brought in some food from Bianco's. You know that restaurant?"

She nodded. "Great Italian food."

"It's in the oven. I just need to heat it up."

"Will you stay and have something to eat, Piper?" my dad asked.

Piper looked hesitant. "I probably shouldn't. I'm supposed to be eating with my family in Jersey."

The look of disappointment on my dad's face was obvious. She caught it and so did I. Then Piper immediately changed her tune.

"But you know..." she said. "Bianco's is really too good to pass up. My stomach is growling. So, maybe I can have a little appetizer with you guys?"

"That would be wonderful. And then stay for a piece of your mom's pie before you hit the road."

Dad fiddled with the joystick on the arm of his chair and maneuvered to the table.

She followed him and turned around to flash me a smile. I smiled back.

So much for an uneventful dinner.

Having Piper here made me tense and excited at the same time. It was an odd mix. I was still pretty baffled that she was the same friend Dad had been raving about for the past several days. Her keeping him company made me realize that she really was a genuinely good person. It hadn't been an act.

During dinner, Piper and I snuck glances at each other. I knew there was probably so much she wanted to say to me, that she couldn't in front of my father. Perhaps some of those things contained expletives.

Piper chewed on her seafood lasagna and asked, "So, what do you do, Mason?"

I took a sip of my wine to ponder how I wanted to answer that and finally said, "I'm an entrepreneur."

My father was just about to open his big mouth when I diverted the conversation before he could start to tell her more about me.

Snapping my fingers, I said, "Hey, Dad. Did you tell Piper about your surgery?"

A look of concern crossed her face. "What surgery?"

My father downplayed it. "No big deal. Just gonna finally get my hip replaced. Been needing to for a long time, and I'm stuck in this chair until my leg gets stronger anyway."

"Oh wow. When?"

"Next month."

I broke apart a piece of bread. "I've been trying to convince him to let me move him in with me for a while, but he won't budge."

"I'm most comfortable in my apartment. It's simple, and I know where everything is."

She sighed. "Well, depending on how you feel, Mr. Hanks, it might be better to be where your son can look after you at night for a little while."

My eyes locked with hers when I said, "Thank you. I agree."

Well, that was a win. I'd somehow diverted the topic of my job and got Piper on my side when it came to my father's post-op situation to boot.

After dinner, I poured some more wine for us as we devoured the pumpkin pie Piper had brought. True to form, after any amount of alcohol, my father literally conked out in his seat. His head bent back and he began to snore.

"Is he okay?" she asked.

"You do hear that, right? He's more than breathing. He's fine. It's what he does when he has the slightest amount of alcohol."

"Okay. Well, you would know."

I took her empty pie plate over to the counter. "Can I cut you another slice?"

She held out her hand. "No. I'm done. Thank you."

"The pie was delicious. Thank your mother for the recipe."

Piper looked a little sad. "Oh...I wish I could. My mom is dead."

Great. Good one, Mason.

"I'm sorry. I feel like an ass now."

"Well, an ass would be your norm, wouldn't it?" She winked.

I exhaled and stared at her in silence for a few moments. "I probably deserve that." Returning to the table, I pulled out my chair and sat down. "How long has your mother been gone?"

"She died a decade ago of uterine cancer."

"I'm sorry."

"I've always been more diligent about my own health as a result. A year ago, I was actually diagnosed with an early stage of the same type of cancer." She swallowed. "Because it was detected early, I was able to get it taken care of. But unfortunately, that means I can't have kids."

Her admission knocked the wind out of me. That was some pretty heavy stuff to tell a virtual stranger. And I felt awful that she had been through that. But I commended her for being so candid. *What do I even say?*

"I'm glad to hear you'll be okay."

"When you experience a health scare like that, it changes your entire outlook. At least for me it did. It's why I've tried to do good for people, why I switched from a corporate job to interior design, which is my passion. I'm still trying to get on my feet in that arena...but I'm getting there. So, a lot of good came from my diagnosis, too."

I felt like a million unsaid words were choking me. I really needed to somehow explain my actions that first day. I'd really wanted to address it from the moment she walked in the door, but there hadn't been an appropriate time until now. Not to mention, she'd just opened up to me in a pretty big way. I could do the same.

"Piper...I need to apologize to you for my behavior that day. I honestly don't know what came over me."

"You don't have to—"

"No. I need to. Hear me out."

She nodded and let me speak.

"I'd been visiting dad, trying to get his sink to stop leaking—because I hate hiring anyone for something I can do myself. It's not about the money. It's just the way I've always been. I'd just gotten some bad news about a work-related issue and had gone outside for a breather and a cigarette. I shouldn't have been smoking, because I'd quit."

I continued, "Anyway, when you came over to me, I wasn't in my right mind. I immediately put a label on you that wasn't even correct. When you assumed I was home-less, in that moment, it was like I'd gone back in time for a second. You'd turned into every stuck-up rich kid in school who'd ever teased me growing up for coming in with ripped clothing. I came from the opposite side of the tracks, and I guess a part of me must still feel self-conscious about people's perceptions of me. It doesn't matter whether you're a self-made success story now or not, that shit sticks with you. And unfortunately, Piper, you got caught up in my knee-jerk reaction. I'm very sorry."

She smiled. "So...once you realized you were in the wrong, how did buying me a bag of dildos become the next logical step?"

"Fair question. Believe it or not, that was my attempt at an apology."

She bent her head back in laughter. "I don't know... saying 'I'm sorry for overreacting' might have worked just as well?"

"That wouldn't have been as fun to execute." I laughed. "It was my mother who actually taught me that humor was a cure-all for most things. That was my attempt at honoring her."

"With a bag of dicks..."

I shrugged. "I suppose."

She let out a deep sigh. "Well, apology accepted."

My eyes stayed fixed on her smile. She had a beautiful smile, so comforting. Now wonder Dad liked her so much.

"Thank you for keeping my father company. I can't be here all of the time. It's nice to know he has good people around looking out for him."

"Honestly, your father has given me a lot of practical advice. I'm just as lucky to have him."

"Oh yeah? What kind of advice has the old geezer given you?"

"Just advice on life...men..."

I cackled. "You're listening to dating advice from an eighty-year-old man?"

"He's very wise. I recently ended a long-term relationship that wasn't right for me. Your father pointed out something that I hadn't even noticed, that Warren's shoes were always perfectly shiny."

"What was the significance of that?" I asked.

"In retrospect, there was a lot about that relationship that wasn't right for me. If I'd noticed the shiny shoes earlier, maybe it would've tipped me off to the fact that Warren was very self-centered and materialistic and wouldn't have been the right person for me. Your dad is very perceptive. He's shared a lot of stories about his relationship with your mom, too. Just really precious stuff."

That made me smile. Thinking about my parents' love for each other always did. It was rare, and I'd honestly given up on ever finding that myself in this lifetime.

I wanted to know more about Piper.

"So, you said you're an interior designer...but that wasn't always your career?"

"No, I was a business analyst. I'd gone to school for business. But after my health scare, I decided it was time to do something I was passionate about. So I started attending interior design school at night and put all of my resources into a new business. I eventually left my old career. I have a couple of design clients who keep me afloat, but I'm still growing."

"Good for you. Not many people have the balls to take the bull by the horns like that."

She tilted her head. "What is it exactly that you do?"

Ugh.

"I...work in real estate."

I wasn't quite sure why I continued to feel the need to be vague. I guess since we were getting along so well,

I didn't want her developing any preconceived notions about me. The way we'd met was bad enough.

She waited a bit for me to elaborate, but then when I didn't, she just said, "I see."

My father suddenly jumped in his chair, waking himself up.

"Well, look who's still alive!" I joked.

He blinked several times "How long was I out this time?"

"About a half-hour."

"Piper still here?"

"I'm right here, Mr. H." She smiled.

He finally turned and saw her.

"My son hasn't scared you away yet, eh?"

"No. We've actually been having a pretty nice conversation." She looked at the clock. "But actually, I should get going. My family is going to wonder where I am."

I put my hands in my pockets, wishing I could have told her to stay. But it was Christmas Eve, and she needed to be with her family.

"Give them my love," he said to her.

She bent down and gave him a hug before he took off to the bathroom.

I walked Piper to the door, and an awkward silence ensued as she lingered just outside the doorway.

"Thank you for dinner," she said

"Thank you for—oh I don't know—let's see. Thank you for not ratting me out as a condescending asshole to my father. Thank you for looking out for said old man over the past several days...also for a nice conversation and a damn good pie to boot."

She leaned in. "Can I tell you a secret?"

"Yeah."

Her breath brushed against my cheek as she said, "I still sort of think you're an asshole."

Shaking my head, I laughed. "You're nothing if not honest, Piper." I lifted my brow. "And you might be right."

She said nothing else before taking off. Her ass wiggled as she walked down the hall. Damn if watching that wasn't the best Christmas gift I could've asked for.

CHAPTER 4

Piper

I hoped it wasn't too early.

I knocked lightly just in case Mr. Hanks was still sleeping. I'd been just about to walk away when I heard the low buzzing noise his electric chair made when it moved.

The door opened.

"Merry Christmas, Mr. H....oh...boy...what happened?" Mr. Hanks's face had a half-dozen pieces of tissue stuck to it.

"Shaving is a bitch still. But Merry Christmas, sweetheart."

His neck still had stubble, and he'd missed a few parts of his face.

"Thank you. Can I come in?"

He pulled the joystick on his wheelchair arm and his chair backed up. "Of course. I was going to come down to see you before I headed out for the day."

Closing the door behind me, I said, "What time is your son coming to pick you up today?"

"Around noon. I figured I'd get an early start because things take a little longer these days."

I smiled. "Could I help you get ready?"

"Are you hitting on me again? First you try to *help me* into bed. Now you want to *help me* get dressed? I told you, I'm too old for you." He winked.

I laughed. "I meant help you shave."

"There's an art to shaving a man's face. I have shaky hands, but that might be better than you thinking my neck is like your legs."

"I actually used to shave my grandfather all the time. He had Alzheimer's, and toward the end, he didn't get out of bed. He also didn't talk much. So that's what I would do when I visited him every week. I'd give him a nice shave and tell him all about my day. It made me feel useful, and it was better than just staring at him like most people who came to visit did."

Mr. Hanks shrugged. "Alrighty then. I'll take you up on that offer. If Mason sees a slice in my throat from shaving, he'll have an aide here around the clock, instead of just the eight hours a day the one he hired annoys me."

I laughed and pushed Mr. Hanks down the hall to the bathroom. "Your son is protective of you. I have to admit, he's pretty different than the person I originally thought he was."

"Yeah. Mason...well...he can be a bit of an ass. But he's come a long way. When my wife and I first brought him home, he got suspended three times in the first year...and he was only in fourth grade."

"Brought him home?"

"Yeah, Mason's adopted. I thought I'd mentioned that."

That was something I'd definitely remember. "No, I don't think so."

"My wife and I couldn't have kids. Mason was nine when we brought him home. He was constantly getting in trouble for being disruptive in class. Halfway through the year, we figured out why. He was in fourth grade but could do the math work of a high school senior. Kid was a genius and social services had no clue."

"Oh wow." I took the shaving cream out of the medicine cabinet and sprayed a glob onto my hands before lathering up and rubbing it on Mr. Hanks's neck and the places he'd missed on his face. "That's crazy."

"He was living on the streets, so it wasn't like he went to school on a regular basis for anyone to get to know him."

I froze with my hands on Mr. Hanks's neck. "He was... homeless."

"Yeah. It gave him a tough edge. But underneath all that armor is a heart of gold. Trust me, he was the apple of my wife's eye, and he couldn't do enough for her."

God, I felt like a complete idiot now. No wonder he'd gotten so upset when I mistook him for a homeless person.

I finished shaving Mr. Hanks and then wheeled him back to the living room. I knew it was getting late, and I had to go, so I took out the envelope I'd come to give him.

"Merry Christmas, Mr. Hanks. I'll explain it once you open it."

"I have a little something for you, too." He lifted his chin. "There's an envelope on the kitchen counter over there. Could you grab it for me?"

"Of course."

I laughed looking down at the plain white envelope with my name written on it. We'd unknowingly given each other matching gifts.

"You go first," I said.

Mr. Hanks opened the sealed envelope and took out the business card I'd slipped inside. He read it and then looked up at me with his brows knitted. "An old-age home? I hope your gift isn't that you're putting me there."

I laughed. "No, it's definitely not. But that's where I'll be today. The East Side Assisted Living Center has a floor for people living there temporarily while recovering from strokes. I'm serving lunch there today and then playing cards and games with the residents after. I can't really afford gifts, and honestly most of the gifts I'd bought over the years were just unnecessary, so this year I'm donating my time and doing good deeds in honor of people. Today I'll do my best to spread Christmas cheer with you in mind."

It looked like Mr. Hanks started to get a little choked up. He swallowed. "Thank you. That's really kind of you."

I smiled. "My turn now! I tore open the envelope with the excitement of a little kid on Christmas morning. Funny enough, there was a business card inside my gift, too. Mine was for The Lotus—a swanky, five-star hotel that overlooked Central Park."

"Turn it over," he said. "There's a name written on the back."

"Marie Desidario," I said aloud.

Mr. Hanks nodded. "You go see her first thing tomorrow morning. I got a connection with the hotel and happen to know they're planning on redoing all their suites. If you can come up with designs by New Year's Eve, they'll look at your proposal. They already got stuff from some other firm and committed to make their decision by the beginning of the year. But I bet you can knock their socks off."

My eyes bulged from my head. "Oh my, God! That's...I don't even know what to say. That's so incredible. Landing a job like The Lotus Hotel could be career changing. I...I....I'm going to hug you. But I promise I'm *not* hitting on you."

VI KEELAND & PENELOPE WARD

Mr. Hanks chuckled as I engulfed him in a giant hug. I seriously couldn't believe I was going to get a chance to submit my designs to a place like that.

"Merry Christmas, sweetheart."

"Merry Christmas to you, too, Mr. H. And tell your son I hope he has a nice holiday, too."

"You bet."

Over the next five days, I had to have drunk five gallons of coffee. I'd called Marie at The Lotus bright and early the day after Christmas, and she told me to stop by so she could give me the specs she'd supplied to the other vendors. While I was there, she also gave me a tour of the hotel and the suites I'd be providing designs for. I'd been to the hotel once with Warren for dinner, but I'd never seen it at Christmas time. The place was truly magical.

I stood in the lobby with my large portfolio bag slung over my shoulder and looked around in awe. For inspiration, I'd stopped by every day since I met with Marie the first time, yet each time I stepped into the magnificent lobby I couldn't help but be overwhelmed by its beauty. In my heart, I felt unworthy of the opportunity to design anything for this place, even though I truly did love the concepts I came up with.

I rode the elevator up to the 6th floor where the business offices were located and knocked on the manager's open door before entering. Marie smiled warmly.

"Come in, Piper. It's good to see you." She extended her hand from behind her desk.

"You, too." I wiped my hand on my pants before stepping forward to shake. "Sorry. I'm a nervous wreck. I don't want to sweaty palm you."

Marie smiled. "There's nothing to be nervous about. Why don't you have a seat?" There was a small round table with a few chairs in the corner of her office, and she motioned in that direction. "We can spread out over there better."

Over the next hour and a half, I showed Marie my concepts. I'd made two very different boards to present, but honestly I liked one much better than the other. Marie clearly agreed. She *oohed* and *aahed* at the rich fabric I'd chosen for the window dressings and told me the loved the uniqueness and quality of the hand-painted cherry blossoms wallpaper I'd suggested. Overall, I thought the presentation couldn't have gone any better.

"Well, I'll be meeting with the owner this afternoon. He's seen the other concepts already. I'll make my recommendation to him, but ultimately the final choice is his. So I don't want to get your hopes up, but yours is my new favorite."

"Really?"

She nodded. "Really."

I was so excited that the professional demeanor I'd been trying to portray flew right out the window. I jumped up out of my seat and threw my arms around her for a hug. "Thank you so much!"

She laughed. "You're welcome. But I guess my telling you not to get your hopes up didn't really help, did it?"

"No, I guess not. But I do understand that my designs might not get picked. Honestly, it's just been a dream to even come here and get a chance to present to you. Whatever happens, I'll always be grateful for the opportunity."

"Mr. Hanks said you were something special. I can understand why now."

"Thank you. I didn't realize you'd met him. He said he knew the owner, so I wasn't sure."

Marie smiled. "Yes, he definitely knows the owner. He comes by quite a bit, actually. Though not as much lately."

"Yeah, it's definitely harder for him to get around these days. But I'm taking him out to lunch this afternoon...to say thank you for getting me the chance to present to you. I've been neglecting him while I worked the last week, and I want to celebrate with him."

"Have a great time. And I'll be in touch within the next few days, one way or the other."

On the way out of the hotel, I saw a homeless man on the curb outside. I dug into my pocketbook and, unfortunately, I only had ten bucks. Without thinking, I went to hand it to him, but then I remembered the last time I'd rushed to help a person whom I thought was homeless...I'd wound up with a bag full of dicks.

Which...as twisted as it was, I'd been seriously considering digging into to thoughts of the not-homeless man who gave it to me.

God, Mason was handsome.

I sighed.

This time, before I got myself into trouble again, I walked over to the man. "Hi. Are you...waiting for a cab?"

The guy's face was dirty, and his hair clearly hadn't been washed in a long time. He looked at me like I was nuts. "No, I'm waiting for Cinderella to swing by and pick me up for the ball. Jesus, lady, go away...unless you want to buy me something to eat."

I smiled and extended the ten dollars to him. "Actually. I'd love to buy you lunch. Have a Happy New Year."

He shook his head, but quickly grabbed the bill from my hand. "Yeah. You, too."

That evening, I was about to get changed when there was a knock at my door. My heart started to race as I looked through the peephole.

"Mason. Is...everything alright with your dad?"

"Yeah. Yeah. Everything is fine."

My hand covered my heart. "You scared me."

"Sorry about that. I was just wondering..." he looked down. "If you'd like to have dinner."

"You mean me, you, and your dad, right?"

He flashed a boyish smile. "No. I mean just me and you."

"Like a date?"

He chuckled. "Yes, exactly like a date. You know why?"

"Why?"

"Because it *would be a date*, Piper."

"Oh! Wow. Ummm. I..."

"Did you have plans?"

"Well, it is New Year's Eve. So, yes, I did have plans."

Mason squinted. "And those plans are?"

"I have a date with two men."

His brows shot up.

I smirked. "Ben and Jerry. I was just going to sit at home and watch the ball drop while eating Chunky Monkey."

Mason shook his head. "Be ready at eight."

My hands went to my hips. "No. Not when you say it like that."

He rolled his eyes. "Do you or don't you want to go out with me?"

"I guess I do. But I want better than *be ready at eight*. God, you can really be an asshole."

We glared at each other. Eventually, he broke the stare off. "Piper. Would you please be ready at eight o'clock tonight?"

I smirked. "How about eight fifteen?

He grumbled '*What the hell am I doing*' under his breath and turned to walk away. "I'll see you later."

I walked out into the hall. "Wait! Where are we going? What should I wear?"

"Wear whatever you want."

"But what will you be wearing?"

He still didn't turn around. "Whatever *I* want."

"Are we taking public transportation? I'll need to know for shoe selection."

Mason arrived at the elevator bank and pushed the button. "We won't be taking public transportation."

"What about outer wear? Will I need a hat and gloves?"

The elevator doors slid open. He looked down the hall at me before stepping in. "Sure, bring them. Bring anything you want. Even your bag of dicks is welcome. See you at eight, Piper."

And then...just like that, he was gone.

Right at eight, there was a knock at my door. Expecting it to be Mason, I opened it looking down at my dress. "I don't know if what I'm wearing is too dressy...*oh*." I looked up. "I'm sorry, I thought you were Mason."

The older man took off his hat and nodded. "I'm Mr. Mason's driver, ma'am. He asked me to collect you at eight."

Driver?
Collect me?

I was thoroughly confused. "You mean Mason isn't here?"

"No, ma'am. He had some work to attend to, so he asked me to pick you up."

"Oh...well. That's...okay. I guess if he's stuck at work. Let me just grab my bag. Come in."

The driver smiled. "I'll just wait out here."

"Suit yourself." I grabbed my purse and checked out my reflection in the mirror one last time. I'd picked out a beaded black dress since it was New Year's Eve. But I thought I might have been overdressed. So when I went into the hall, I asked the driver. "Would you know if what I'm wearing is okay? I mean...do you know how nice the restaurant is he's taking me to?"

"It's a very nice restaurant."

"Is it *beaded dress* nice?"

The man smiled. "Yes, I think so."

I sat in the back of a Lincoln Town Car for almost forty-five minutes as the driver navigated through heavy city traffic. This was already a strange date...from the way we'd argued when he asked me out to dinner, to him sending his driver instead of showing up himself. But I was definitely excited. Mason Hanks was absolutely gorgeous, and despite his edge of arrogance, he was funny, and I liked that we had good banter. So I had butterflies in my stomach the entire drive.

The car slowed to a stop in front of where I'd been earlier, The Lotus Hotel. I was confused until I saw the man standing out front waiting, while fiddling with an oversized watch.

Wow. Mason looked great in a suit. The way it fit his broad shoulders and hugged his arms, it had to have been custom fitted. His hair was slicked back, and he stood with his feet planted wide, looking very impatient. I don't know why, but the fact that he looked like he was annoyed tickled me. Mason looked up and our eyes caught. He smiled and I nearly lost it. *Oh my.* He looked...well, drop dead gorgeous...like an old-time movie star.

Leaning down to the car, he opened the door and extended a hand. "It's about time."

"I don't control traffic, you know."

The corner of his lip twitched. He looked me up and down. "You look beautiful."

I softened. "Thanks. You don't look so bad yourself."

He folded his arm and offered me his elbow.

"I was just here this afternoon. Did you know that your dad is friends with the owner, and he got me a chance to present some designs for a redecorating project?"

Mason nodded. "I did know that."

A doorman opened the door with a nod as we approached.

Inside, even though I'd been here six times in six days, the grand beauty again overwhelmed me. I looked up in awe. "God, I love this hotel."

Mason smiled. "That's good. Because you're going to be spending a lot of time in the bedrooms upstairs."

"You're awfully sure of yourself." The more his comment sank in, the more it annoyed me. "You know what, you have a lot of nerve assuming that just because I agreed to go on a date with you, I'll be jumping into bed with you."

Mason started to laugh. "Calm your pits, Piper."

His comment pissed me off even more. "No. I will not calm my pits. I don't care how good looking you are, I'm not going to date an asshole."

Mason's smile was so smug. "You think I'm good looking."

I rolled my eyes. "Figures an *asshole* would not hear the part about him *being an asshole*."

"You're really cute when you're mad."

I squinted at him. "You're unbelievable." Maybe that driver was still outside and could take me back home. "You know what? I'm out of here. Unfortunately, the apple *does* fall far from the tree sometimes. I have no idea how your dad could be so sweet and you could be such a jerk. But goodbye, Mason."

I turned on my heel to storm out when Mason grabbed my arm.

"Wait."

"What?"

"I'm not really that big of a jerk. I can explain."

"Oh yeah? You can explain how you're not a jerk for assuming I would jump into bed with you. This might be worth sticking around to hear."

Mason smiled. "When I said you were going to be spending a lot of time in the bedrooms, I meant you would be working. You got the contract for the suites, Piper."

My face wrinkled. "What?"

"I *own* The Lotus Hotel...and a few others."

"What are you talking about?"

"When you mentioned you were an interior designer the other night, I told my dad to give you the card with Maria's number for me. I figured I'd give you a shot. You were kind to my father, and I like to make sure kindness is repaid."

"So you gave me a multi-million dollar contract because I was nice to your dad?"

"No. You got the shot, because of my dad. You earned the contract. You had the best presentation, fair and square. Even Maria recommended your designs."

I should've been thrilled to have scored a major job like this, but instead I felt deflated. My chest was heavy. "Oh. Okay. Thanks, I guess."

Mason's forehead wrinkled. "What's wrong? You don't look happy?"

"I am. It's just..." I shook my head. "Nothing."

"Spit it out, what's going on in that head of yours?"

"I guess...I thought...well, I thought this was a date."

He squinted. "It is a date."

"No, I mean a *date date*. Not a business dinner thing."

Mason looked back and forth between my eyes. Cupping both my cheeks, he lowered his face to mine. Before I could register what was about to transpire, he crushed his lips to mine, swallowing the gasp of shock I let out. At first, I could merely try to keep up, opening when he opened, offering my tongue when his pilfered my mouth, clutching him when he'd already had me in his clutches. But eventually, all thought slipped away and instinct took over. I kissed him even harder, pressed my body against his, and sucked on his tongue. Mason growled. The sound shot through me, traveling down to between my legs with a ripple.

His hands at my cheeks slid to behind my neck, and he tilted my head to deepen the kiss. We made out for a solid ten minutes standing in the middle of a busy lobby, yet I'd felt like we were all alone in a room. When we finally broke, we were both panting.

"Wow," I said.

Mason smiled. "It's a fucking date, Piper."

I smiled back. "It's a date. But you're still an asshole."

❧

A few weeks later we were inseparable.

Things had moved really fast between the two of us. We'd spent six nights a week together, a few of those alone, and a few with his dad. Friday, I'd even fallen asleep at his house, but we still hadn't *slept together*. Though I was hoping that would change tonight.

After I made us dinner, Mason helped me take down the Christmas decorations. He dragged my half-dead tree downstairs to put out for tomorrow's garbage, while I vacuumed up all the bristles that fell off.

"Thank you for taking that out," I said when he came back. "I hate doing that job."

"No problem."

"Could I bother you to do one more thing for me?"

He wiggled his brows. "Only if I can bother you to do one thing for me later."

I laughed. He teased a lot, but Mason hadn't pressured me *at all* about sex, even though we'd fooled around a bit. That only made me want him even more.

"I have another bag for you to take down to the garbage," I said. "Hang on, let me go grab it."

I went into the bedroom and took out the brown paper bag I'd stuffed into a drawer. I have no idea why, but I'd kept everything, even the original bag. I took a deep breath and walked back out to find Mason watching some football game on TV. "Here you go. I won't be needing these anymore."

Mason had been staring at the TV, but when he saw the bag I was holding out, he turned with interest. With a curious look, he took the bag and opened it.

"It's your bag of dicks. How can you get rid of this?"

"I was hoping to trade it for the real thing?"

Mason's eyes darkened. "Are you saying what I think you're saying?"

I smiled. "I want you, Mason. Like *now*."

One minute I was standing there holding out the bag, and the next I was scooped up into Mason's arms. "What my girl wants, my girl gets."

My girl. I really liked that. I smiled and leaned my head against his shoulder as he started to march toward my bedroom. "What about the bag, don't' you want to toss it out?"

"Nope." He kissed me. "You can have all this *and* a bag of dicks. You're one lucky girl."

THE END

Merry Christmas to our Readers!
We hope you get a bag of dicks and more
under your tree this year!

KISSMAS IN
NEW YORK

CHAPTER 1

Margo

Nancy spoke over the loud sound of steaming milk. "I can't believe they bailed on us."

"Really? Because I can."

I'd just gotten a text from my soon-to-be ex-husband saying he and his lawyer couldn't make it for our meeting...the meeting that was supposed to start five minutes ago. This was the second time he'd done this to me, claiming to be swamped at work. We'd even scheduled the appointment today at a café near his office in Soho to accommodate him, because he'd complained it took too long to get to either of our attorney's offices. Not only that, I'd had to ask my best friend Nancy to fill in for my own lawyer when my regular divorce attorney got into a car accident yesterday. That's how desperate I was to get today over with. If I bent anymore for the asshole, I'd break in half.

"Well, you know what I mean. I can *believe* it," Nancy said. "But, man, the balls on Rex!"

It was just after Thanksgiving and already starting to look a lot like Christmas. The whole café was decked out in white lights and garland. I'd been hopeful when I walked in, thinking maybe the cheerful atmosphere would offset the misery of the meeting. But of course, anything involving Rex doesn't end well.

I tried to make the best of it, opting to enjoy the seasonal eggnog latte, which I looked forward to every year. Holiday cheer *should've* been in the air, aside from the fact that my Scrooge of an ex—Rex—had pulled his usual crap. I'd agreed to a simple, no-fault divorce—which was ironic since the entire demise of my marriage was his fault—yet he needed a sit-down meeting. One apparently he and his lawyer decided not to show up for. That was just like him, unfortunately.

So, for the past hour, I'd been hanging out with Nancy, my childhood best friend. I normally tried not to mix business with pleasure, but she seemed eager and up to the task, and I was desperate not to delay this divorce anymore than Rex already had.

Mariah Carey's "All I Want For Christmas" played low on the overhead speaker. I always loved this time of year; if only I didn't have the dark cloud of these divorce proceedings looming over me, I could have truly enjoyed it.

Nancy drank down the last of her latte. "We need to figure out a way to spice up your life. Seriously, you do nothing but work and stress over this damn divorce. That can't be healthy. Why don't you come to my firm's holiday party with me? It's a harbor cruise."

"I don't know. I'll think about it."

"Even better...maybe we can go away somewhere after the New Year."

Only half listening to her, I checked my phone. "Maybe." A ton of emails had come in while I'd been at the café.

My job as one of the top event planners in Manhattan kept me super busy. Whether I was planning posh parties in the Hamptons or galas in the city, my schedule was chock full, seven days a week.

Nancy snapped her fingers in front of my face. "Did you hear me? I said maybe we should go away after the holidays."

I forced myself to put my phone away. "Where would we go if we went away?"

She pursed her lips. "You know...I'm not sure I'll even tell you. It'll be a surprise. You can find out when we get on the plane. Your whole life is planned and scheduled in your damn phone. Pretty sure I'm going to make you get rid of that for a week, too."

As if on cue, my text notification chimed, prompting me to take my phone out again and check it. It was one of the vendors for a holiday party I was in charge of. The thought of ever parting with my phone gave me the shakes.

"Don't be ridiculous. I could never be without my phone for a week."

"You don't have an impulsive bone in your body. You need to unplug and live a little before your entire life passes you by."

Playing with my empty cup, I said, "Impulsivity is a choice. I can be impulsive if I want to."

She looked skeptical. "Really..."

"Yes."

"So, if I dared you to do something right now in this café that you would never normally choose to do—anything at all—you would do it on a whim...for the sake of impulsivity?"

I saw where this was going. Nancy's little dares went back to our childhood in Queens. It had all started in fifth grade when I'd tried to dare her to tell Kenny Harmon she liked him. But I never even got the words out...I'd said, "I dare you to..." and crazy Nancy cut me off and exclaimed, "I'll do it!" What followed was ten years of us accepting each other's dares before knowing what they were. I'd done so many things I would never have done otherwise—skinny-dipping, asking the most gorgeous guy in school to the prom, bungee jumping. I had to admit, some of those dares turned out to be some of the best times I'd ever had. But it had been a long time since we'd played our little game.

Though...what could she possibly have me do that was so drastic anymore? Of course, it would also totally prove her point that I couldn't be impulsive if I said no. And...I did hate to break our long-running streak of agreeing to those silly dares.

I sat up straight. "Yeah. Sure. Why not?"

She lifted her brow. "You're absolutely sure?"

I hesitated, then answered, "Yes."

How old am I?

What am I getting myself into?

Her assertion that I wasn't adventurous had me sort of pissed—mostly at myself— because she was right. I really couldn't back out now. Even though Nancy and I had been playing games like this since we were kids, it wasn't exactly cute anymore as adults. But when she put her mind to something in order to prove a point, she didn't let up. It was partly why she was such a good lawyer. Not sure if it was because Rex ruined my day for the umpteenth time, putting me in a shit mood, but for some reason, I just didn't feel like letting her win this time.

Wanting to get it over with, I asked, "So what's my torture going to be?"

She closed her eyes for a bit. "I'm thinking. It has to be good...something that I truly don't think you'll actually do."

Now she was really getting on my nerves. Whatever it was...I was going to have to go with it—just to prove her wrong.

After a minute of whatever weird meditation thing she was doing to concentrate, she finally said, "Okay. I've decided what it is. But you're lucky, because I'm going to let you choose part of it."

"Explain."

"I want you to kiss a stranger. Someone in this coffee shop."

What?

"Are you kidding me?"

"Not at all...but you'll get to choose who it is. I'm not that cruel to make you kiss just anyone." She whispered and nudged her head. "Like him."

The old man next to us had grease from his egg sandwich dribbling down his chin.

Knowing she wouldn't back down from this idea, I sighed and muttered, "Fine."

"What was that? I couldn't hear you?"

I gritted my teeth. "Fine!"

"Great. Who's it gonna be?" Nancy's eyes wandered around the room, then landed on someone in the corner. "Yes." She beamed. "Ohhhh, yes. Yes. Yes! Today is your lucky day. I can't believe I hadn't noticed him sooner." She squinted. "Doesn't look like he's wearing a wedding ring, either, so score."

I braced myself, then turned around to see whom she was looking at.

She had to be kidding me.

The distinguished-looking, dark-haired man sitting in the corner was drop-dead gorgeous, dressed to the nines in a three-piece suit that looked like it was tailor-made for his perfect physique. His nose was buried in *The New York Times*. It was a perfect nose that complemented his perfect jaw-line. Have I mentioned he was *perfect*?

This guy would laugh in my face!

There was no way I was going to embarrass myself in front of him. The choice had to be a happy medium... someone I wouldn't mind making a fool of myself in front of—but he also couldn't be hideous.

"Okay, who's it going to be?" she said, looking down at the time on her phone. "I think I'm going to run to get some Christmas shopping done since Rex bailed. So let's get this show on the road."

My eyes perused the room.

The young mom in the corner with her baby? Nope.

The teenage barista boy? Um...pretty sure I'd get arrested.

Oh my God.

There was literally no one else aside from the old man and Mr. Perfect.

I reassessed.

The dribbler next to us? No way. I just couldn't do it, not even on my best day.

It came back to Mr. Perfect. He'd won by default.

"You're right. He's the only viable option." I blew a frustrated breath up into my dirty blonde hair. "The guy is going to think I'm a nutjob."

"Not if you explain yourself properly. It's up to you as to how you spin it."

"If I do this, I get to prove a point. But what's in it for you?"

"Either I get to prove myself right, or I get to have a little fun. Either way, I win. Besides, I think it's actually good for you. When's the last time those lips have been touched anyway?"

I couldn't even remember. That was sad. Honestly, I hadn't kissed anyone since my cheating ex, Rex. (Yes, Rex rhymes with ex, and I should've taken it as an omen before I ever said 'I do'.)

Taking a deep breath in, I got up. "I'm going to get this over with."

My footsteps couldn't have moved any slower. I kept looking back at Nancy as she watched me intently. My heart raced. The poor guy was oblivious as to what was about to happen.

Madonna's rendition of "Santa Baby" played in the background as I made my way slowly over to him.

I found myself even more paralyzed the closer I got to his beautiful face.

Stopping right in front of him, I froze.

He turned his head away from what he was reading when he noticed me standing there. "Can I help you?" Of course, his sexy voice matched his exterior.

My nerves suddenly got the best of me as I stammered, "Hi...I'm Margo?"

It came out like a question. *Margo?* Like I didn't even know my own damn name.

He closed his newspaper. "Hi."

I just stood there and continued to say nothing.

"Is...everything alright?" he asked.

Sort of feeling like I was going to piss my pants, I said, "I don't usually do things like this...um..."

He was just squinting at me now. This man thought I was an idiot. I couldn't blame him.

"Are you okay?" he asked.

Laughing exaggeratedly, I said, "Oh my God, yes. Everything is great." I turned around to look at my friend. She was giving me the thumbs-up, egging me on to continue.

"Is it okay if I sit?" I did so before he could even say yes or no. My chair skidded against the wooden floor.

"Uh...yeah. Go right on ahead."

Clasping my fingers together, I smiled at him.

He finally lifted his brow in question, which served as my cue to say something.

Push it out.

"I'm sorry I'm acting so strangely. You're going to think this is crazy." I pointed back to Nancy. "My friend over there...we've known each other since we were kids. She and I have always had these funny bets over the years. Anyway, she just basically accused me of not having a spontaneous bone in my body. I didn't like that. It made me a little angry, actually." I licked my lips. "You seem like a successful guy. I'm sure you know what it feels like to be competitive."

He glanced over at Nancy, then back at me, still looking confused as he said, "Okay..."

"Well...she's not entirely right about me. Just because someone chooses to live responsibly the majority of the time, that doesn't mean they aren't capable of having fun." I was totally rambling and needed to get to the point. "Anyway, she got me to agree to a blind bet, where I would basically agree in advance to do whatever she directed me to—to prove my spontaneity. That's why I'm here."

"She told you to go up to a stranger and start babbling..."

I cringed. "Not exactly."

"What then?"

"I'm supposed to...kiss you."

He didn't respond aside from narrowing his eyes.

Great.

Laughing nervously, I said, "I told you it was crazy."

He finally spoke. "What do you *get* for kissing me?"

"Nothing. I just get to prove that I'm...adventurous."

Silence lingered in the air for a few seconds before he suddenly got up.

Lovely. I've scared him off.

"Where are you going?"

"If we're going to kiss, I should at least buy you a coffee. What do you drink?"

Oh. *Oh.* My heart sped up. *This is going to happen, then?*

"I already had a latte, but thank you."

He continued to the counter anyway, and after a few minutes returned with the most hideous green drink I'd ever laid eyes on. It was in a gigantic cup with a candy cane straw and had what looked like red sparkles immersed throughout. Pretty sure I got a cavity, or diabetes, from just looking at it.

"What is that?"

"It's their iced Christmas tree-ccino. Bought it for my nephew last season. Kept him on a sugar high for three days." He handed it to me. "Tell you what, if you can drink all of this down, we can kiss."

"What's the point of making me drink this first?"

"Well, it's going to take you a while because it's so sweet. That will give us enough time to at least get to know each other properly before I'm supposed to apparently shove my tongue down your throat. But mostly, it will amuse me to watch you drink it. Bonus?" He looked over in Nancy's direction. "Your friend looks really confused right about now. Serves her right, if you ask me."

"That *is* sort of a bonus," I said, looking back at her and smiling. "Alright. It's a deal."

Taking the first sip, I tried to down it fast without really tasting it. Unexpectedly, I got brain freeze and had to stop. "Ugh!" I rubbed my forehead.

He chuckled. "You okay?"

Coughing, I said, "Yup." I slid the cup toward him. "Want a sip? It tastes like Juniper—like a Christmas tree. Maybe a little hint of sap."

"I'm good." He held out his palm. "So..." he said. "What do you do for fun when you're not propositioning strangers in coffeehouses, Margo?"

"I...." Sadly, I couldn't remember the last fun thing I'd done. My shoulder's slumped realizing Nancy was absolutely right—I had no life anymore. "I work a lot. I'm pretty much married to the job."

"Job is a lucky man." There was a hint of a glimmer in his eyes. It was the first time I realized that maybe he wasn't totally turned off by my ludicrous request for a kiss.

Jesus. My nerves had consumed me so much that I hadn't even asked *his* name.

"I'm sorry...I didn't get your name?"

"Chet."

"It's nice to meet you." I took another long sip of the drink, and once again, it went straight to my head.

"I'd slow down on that if I were you. My nephew was bouncing off the walls. Wouldn't want you to do anything to embarrass yourself."

"Pretty sure I'm already there. But thanks."

We shared a smile.

"You know what?" he said. "I admire your willingness to step out of your comfort zone."

"Well, just think of the story you can tell your colleagues when you get back to the office."

He laughed, showcasing his beautiful smile before his phone rang.

Chet looked down. "Shit. I have to take this." He held up his index finger. "One second."

I continued to sip the sickeningly sweet drink while he spoke on the phone. The tone of the call seemed urgent.

When he hung up, I asked, "Is everything okay?"

"Bit of a crisis back at the office. I'm gonna have to head out, unfortunately."

Disappointment washed over me. *This wasn't going to happen after all.* "Oh...okay. We can just forget about the whole thing, then."

I stood up as he did the same.

I held my hand out. "It was nice meeting you."

He took my hand, but instead of shaking it, he suddenly pulled me toward him. The next thing I knew, I felt the friction of his warm lips enveloping mine.

Everything went oddly silent, like the world just stopped as I became immersed in his taste, in his smell.

When his tongue first slipped inside my mouth, it was gentle. Within seconds, it became demanding as something inexplicable ignited between us. Soon, our tongues were colliding. We might have just met, but this just felt right—like I was made to do this.

My fingers raked through his silky, thick hair, touching this man freely as if we'd known each other for months, not mere minutes. The baritone groan of pleasure that exited his lips vibrated through me and made my body quiver.

I didn't even know this guy, and yet suddenly, all I wanted in life was to continue doing this. You just know a man who could use his tongue like that for a kiss, could use it in other amazing ways. Couldn't say I'd ever gotten wet from just a kiss before now.

He suddenly pulled away. His eyes were hazy. Both of us were out of breath.

I wanted more.

Come back.

I stammered, "That was…"

He sighed deeply. "Yeah…"

Holy hell. That kiss was amazing.

After a bit of awkward laughter, we looked around and noticed that all eyes were on us. Nancy's mouth was hanging open.

"Can I call you sometime?" he asked.

Not even having to give it a second thought, I said, "I would love that."

He handed me his phone. "Enter your number for me?"

Flustered, I typed it as fast as I could, as if maybe I was going to wake up from this dream before I had a chance to add all the digits in and he'd disappear into thin air.

"I wish I didn't have to run like this. But I'll call you soon."

"Good luck with whatever you have to deal with."

"Pretty sure I might be a little distracted the rest of the day."

I felt my face heat up.

Me too.

He winked. "Bye." He was just out the door when he turned around and said, "It was like kissing my Christmas tree, by the way."

I'd forgotten that my tongue must have tasted like that hideous green drink. "Bye…Chet," I whispered to myself after he was already gone.

When I returned to the table, Nancy was fanning herself. "That was…interesting. Holy shit."

"Yeah." I smiled. "That was…it was…he was…" The words escaped me.

She was utterly amused. "Look at you. I've never seen you like this."

I mindlessly sipped on the remainder of my green drink. "Pretty sure I've never *felt* like this."

CHAPTER 2

Margo

Nancy and I were sitting on the steps of the courthouse, waiting. I lifted my chin to the coffee truck at the corner that we'd just bought two coffees from. "I dare you to go inside and start taking orders."

The owner had stepped out a minute ago to run into the store across the street. He hung a sign that said *Back in Two Minutes*, but a line started to form as people waited for him to return.

"Oh my God. I could get arrested."

"Good thing you're a lawyer, then."

She gulped back the contents of her Styrofoam coffee cup and stood. "I guess I owe you one since the kissing bandit never called you." She sighed. "I had such high hopes for him."

Her and me both. I'd checked my phone every hour for the days that followed that amazing kiss. I thought for sure hot coffee guy would call me—the chemistry had been off the charts. At least I'd thought so. But the jerk never did.

I watched as Nancy approached the food truck, looked around, then slipped inside. A few seconds later, she had a little notepad in her hand and waved to me from the window as she took her first order. I couldn't stop laughing watching her make coffees and collect money from people. Although my cackling came to a halt when I heard the owner yelling from across the street. He held out a hand to stop cars from crossing, nearly getting himself run over.

"*Shit.*" I stood.

Nancy disappeared from the window just as the owner ran around to the back of the truck. By the time I got to them, she already had the situation under control.

"Thanks, Ahmed." She leaned forward and kissed the man's cheek.

He groaned and climbed into his truck. "You stay in courtroom. Keep out of truck!"

I laughed. "What the hell happened?"

She shrugged. "Nothing. I told him I was a solo practitioner like him, and we had to stick together and help each other out."

"I swear. Only you could have me hysterically laughing on the day I'm coming to court for my final divorce proceeding."

Nancy looked at the time on her phone. "Shit. We better get going. Judge Halloran is a stickler for time."

The security line to get inside was a mile long. Guess everyone decided today was a good day to get divorced. Nancy went through the attorney line so that she could at least be there when the case was called. It took me a solid fifteen minutes until I made my way to the right courtroom on the second floor. The door was closed, and when I opened it, the judge looked right at me. I froze in place, and every head swung in my direction. It felt like a blaring record came to a screeching halt. I thought perhaps I'd walked into the wrong courtroom, but that was definitely our judge sitting up on the bench.

"Can I help you?"

"Ummm. Yes. I mean...I'm supposed to be in here...with my lawyer, for my case this morning."

The judge took off his glasses. "And what time is your calendar call?"

"Calendar call?"

He sighed and looked over at where Nancy was standing. "Miss Lafferty? Did you or did you not inform your client that my court starts at 9:30?"

"Yes, Your Honor. I apologize. The security line was pretty long this morning."

He put his glasses back on and lifted a paper. Nancy caught my eye and motioned for me to get to her table *fast*. The judge didn't bother waiting for me to take my place. He started reading some legal mumbo jumbo as I did my walk of shame. Approaching the gate that separated the players from the spectators, I made the mistake of looking on the other side of the courtroom. My soon-to-be-asshole-ex-husband flashed a phony smile. *Such a dick.* But it was the man standing next to him that made me lose my focus.

And...apparently I needed that focus to put one foot in front of the other. Because as I pushed the little wooden gate open, I lost my balance and tripped.

Shit.

Sprawled out on my ass, I looked up. The judge did not look amused.

The man whom had been the cause of my distraction crouched down next to me and extended a hand to help me up.

I couldn't believe my eyes.

The Adonis from the coffee shop.

The asshole who'd never called.

Was apparently, Rex's lawyer.

I knew his attorney's name: Chester Saint. Never apparently knew he went by *Chet*. I had so many questions. Did he *not* know it was me that day? Or had he been playing some kind of evil game?

He whispered in my ear as he helped me up. "I guess the joke was on me. Karma's a bitch, isn't it?"

Flustered, I stood. Chet—the Kissing Bandit, Esquire—returned to his table, yet I continued to stand there staring at him, dumbfounded. The judge sighed again loudly. "Ms. Adams? If you're not injured, could you possibly take your seat? I think you've made your grand entrance at this point."

I blinked a few times and looked over at Nancy. She gave me a look that said *get the hell over here, you idiot*.

"Ummm. Of course. Sorry about that, Your Honor."

The judge continued. "Mr. Saint? Why are you requesting a continuance today? This is an uncontested divorce, and the asset settlement seems to be in order."

Mr. Saint rose and buttoned his jacket. "Your Honor, we've only just recently found there is a potential discrepancy in the valuation of Ms. Adams' assets, and we need a little bit of time to further investigate the matter."

The judge looked at Nancy. "I take it this is acceptable to you?"

"No, Your Honor."

The judge mumbled, "Of course not."

Nancy motioned to the defendant's table. "I only received the Motion to Continue five minutes ago, when you did, Your Honor. As far as we're concerned, there is no issue on asset valuation. My client and Mr. Adams came to an equitable agreement in good faith."

The judge looked over at the other table. "What seems to be the issue, Mr. Saint?"

"We've been made aware that Ms. Adams has an undisclosed bank account with a substantial sum of money."

I craned my neck out past Nancy to get a good look at my ex. "What? What money? You spent everything we had on that little tart you hired as your secretary—who couldn't *type or answer a phone*, but apparently had *other* skills that met your hiring criteria."

Nancy shushed me.

The judge wasn't as polite. "Ms. Adams. Aside from being on time in my courtroom, you'll also keep quiet unless asked a direct question. Do you understand?"

"But..." Nancy put her hand on my arm, an unspoken warning. I sucked it up. "Yes, Your Honor."

"Since today has been so much fun, let's do it again." The judge put on his glasses and looked down. "Motion for Continuance granted. We'll reconvene three weeks from today." He looked up over the bridge of his glasses. "And be on time, Ms. Adams."

My head was spinning. I had no idea what had just happened. Hot coffee shop guy is my ex's lawyer, and I have hidden assets?

I turned to Nancy. "What the hell?"

"I was about to ask you the same question."

Mr. Saint approached our table with his client and spoke to only Nancy. "We'll need information on the co-owned TD accounts."

She looked to me. "TD accounts? I don't have any accounts at TD Bank." Then it hit me. I glared at Rex. "You mean Nana's accounts? You know those aren't really mine.

They're only jointly titled so that I can go to the bank for her since she's been sick."

Rex said nothing while his attorney glared at me. "We'll need those accounts by the end of the week."

CHAPTER 3

Chet

Two weeks later

Under the glow of dimmed red and green lighting, I stood like a fish out of water in a sea of people—who all looked ridiculous. I'd wanted nothing to do with this holiday party, but one of my biggest clients invited me, so I'd felt obligated to show up. My plan was to show face for an hour, then leave.

It wasn't so much the party I had a problem with. It was the fact that it was Christmas costume-themed, which wasn't really my jam. Who the hell has a costume party in December anyway? I had to get something at the last minute and was none too happy with what I ended up with. Apparently, there were only two costumes in the store big enough for me, and because I'd put it off until the absolute last minute, there had been no time to go anywhere else.

After downing the second Jingle Juice Spiked Punch, my night was starting to seem more promising, though.

That was...until I spotted her.

And it was clear she had noticed me sometime before, because her stare was already burning into mine.

What the hell is she doing here?

Margo.

Margaret Adams.

My client, Rex Adams' soon-to-be ex-wife.

She looked gorgeous as ever. Her long, blonde hair was ombre, darkest at the roots and platinum at the tips. She wore a sexy, long-sleeve red dress with a hint of sparkle, the neckline cut down to her navel. *Christ.* She had on matching high heels, looking every bit like the woman I'd fantasized about for days on end—before I realized who she was.

How the hell did she get out of wearing a costume? Now I wished I hadn't been so stupid to assume coming meant I absolutely had to wear one. Margo looked like a normal human, whereby I was standing here trying to save the last of my dignity while dressed as Buddy the Elf.

I wasn't supposed to have to see her again until our next court date. I still couldn't wrap my head around the fact that Margo from the café—was Margaret Adams.

I glanced over at the door. It was too late to slip out of here because she'd already spotted my ass. The next thing I knew, she was right in front of me.

"Well, well, well, if it isn't Buddy the Kissing Bandit... Chester Saint. Hardly a *saint* if you ask me. More like the devil. What are you doing here?"

"This is my client's holiday party. I was invited. Although, a costume-themed Christmas party is a pretty awful idea."

"Thanks. It was *my* idea. I planned this party."

Shit. I'd forgotten she was an event planner. That explained what she was doing here and why she wasn't dressed like a fool.

She glared at me. "And Carl Rhodes is your client? He's my client, too. Does he realize how crooked you are? That you have no heart?"

I gripped my glass tighter. "Excuse me?"

"Going after my grandmother's money? An eighty-year-old woman's life savings that she uses to pay for her healthcare. You should be ashamed of yourself. If you're such a good detective, how about making yourself useful and going after the money Rex stole from me. I was an idiot to believe the balance of my stocks took such a nose dive last year."

"This is neither the time nor the place to be discussing the case. I don't make a habit of discussing legal matters dressed as Buddy the Elf."

"Really? I think the idiocy suits you well. And it figures Rex would find a lawyer who's as dirty as he is."

Before responding, I downed the rest of my drink, wishing it had quadruple the amount of alcohol. I needed something a fuck of a lot stronger than this spiked jingle juice right about now.

She'd called me crooked? I'd only been doing my job in uncovering those funds connected to her grandmother. I'd never lost a case and didn't intend for this to be the first one. But that didn't mean my clients were always in the right. Rex Adams was not a good person. I'd always known that to be true. And deep down, I'd actually felt bad for his ex—before I actually met her.

But now? I didn't feel bad for her at all. Her calling me crooked was real ironic, considering *she* was the crooked one.

She went on, "Nice of you tell me that day in the café that you represented my husband, by the way."

"You can't be serious. You think I *knew* who you were that day?"

She placed her hands on her hips. "How could you not have?"

"You told me your name was *Margo*. I knew Rex's wife as Margaret. It never occurred to me that you were the same person."

"Margo is my nickname. And I was there with my *attorney* after your client stood me up. What were you even doing there since Rex cancelled our meeting?"

"I was there for the same meeting you were. He called me only a few minutes before you walked over and told me *you* cancelled at the last minute."

"Well, that sounds just like Rex." She leaned forward and squinted at me. "He's a damn *liar*. I would *never* have cancelled. I can't wait to have this divorce finalized."

"Your attorney was also supposed to be a man, according to the documentation I'd had. How would I have known your friend—who sent you on some immature high school dare—was your goddamn lawyer?"

"It was a last-minute change," she muttered.

Shaking my head in disbelief, I said, "Look, I had no clue it was you. I would've never touched you if I'd known."

"So, if you didn't know it was me, then you just get your kicks leading women on?"

What is this woman smoking?

"Leading you on? You approached *me*."

Her tone was filled with emotion. "You never called."

What?

I leaned in. "Kind of hard to call someone who gives you a fake phone number."

Her eyes widened. "What are you talking about?"

"I *did* try to call you—that night. I got some man named Mauricio. He wasn't thrilled when I rang him a second time ten seconds later, either. He confirmed that the number I had was his—not yours."

Margo's eyeballs moved frantically from side to side. "Could I have entered it wrong? Do you still have it...my number in your phone?"

I took my phone out of my pocket and pulled up Margo's name. Not even sure why I hadn't deleted the contact. I turned the screen toward her. She examined the number and frowned, looking genuinely upset.

She cleared her throat. "I typed 4229 when it should have been 4299. I never meant to give you the wrong number."

Well, that's an unexpected plot twist in this fucked-up story.

Softening my stance, I said, "I assumed you were playing some kind of game, one where you go about the city kissing random men and giving them the wrong number for your own enjoyment."

Margo looked deeply into my eyes and said, "I would never do that to someone. What reason would I have had to give you a fake number anyway? That kiss was amazing." Her mouth dropped after that admission, as if her own words had stunned her, like she hadn't expected to be so candid.

I wanted to tell her that I'd done nothing that entire day but think about the way her lips felt on mine, the way her mouth tasted. I dreamt of juniper for days. I hadn't been able to concentrate on anything but her for the longest time. That day, I'd wanted to wait at least twenty-four hours to call her, but ended up biting the bullet and dialing that night, hoping to convince her to meet me. I would've gone anywhere she asked to just to see her again.

But now that I knew *who* she was, how could I admit all that? Even *talking* to her right now was a huge conflict of interest.

"I guess we both got caught up in a big misunderstanding," I finally said.

Her eyes glistened. "So, you *did* try to call me?"

"Yes..." I nodded. "I did."

Margo blinked several times and stared off before looking back up at me. If this situation were different, the realization of this misunderstanding would have been a good thing. But now? Where do we even go from here? We're already at a dead end.

My eyes wandered down to the exposed skin of her plunging neckline, the trail of cleavage that led to the taut, exposed skin below it. I suddenly felt like I had to adjust myself through my yellow spandex. Yeah, this was not a good moment to get excited, not only because my dick was basically in a sock, but because Margo Adams was officially the last woman on Earth I was allowed to feel this way about.

"Look, I don't have anything against you, Margaret. I'm just doing my job in representing Rex."

She blew out a breath. "I understand that. And I'm sure Rex is feeding you lies. He's a liar, Chet." Her voice shook. "He cheated on me. I never did anything to deserve it. All I want is a clean break from that mistake of a marriage, and he's making it so hard for me to just live my life. I won't settle for anything less than a good man whom I can trust."

"You shouldn't have to, Margo," I said without hesitation.

Rex needed his head examined for ever cheating on this woman.

And why had I started calling her *Margo* again? Margo was the woman I'd kissed in the café. The woman in front of me is *Margaret*. My client's wife—who's completely off-limits. That's what I was supposed to believe. But as I continued to look down at her, all I could see was a sweet, beautiful, honest person standing in front of me. And all I wanted to do was something I knew I never could—kiss her again.

"Can I ask you a personal question?" she asked.

"Is it about the case? Honestly, there are rules about talking to a client who is represented. I shouldn't be discussing anything without your attorney present."

She shook her head. "It's not about the case, no. Just a general question."

Technically I just couldn't discuss her case, but really I shouldn't be having a conversation with her at all. My client would blow a gasket if he knew I was making small talk with his ex-wife. No less wanting to lean in and take a giant whiff of her hair.

Shit. Where had that come from? I seriously had the strongest urge to smell her goddamn hair. I needed to end this conversation once and for all. And that's exactly what I'd planned on doing, except the words that came out of my mouth were:

"Sure. What's your question?"

"How do you represent assholes?"

I stifled a laugh. It was about her case, considering Rex seemed like a giant one. Nevertheless, I cleared my throat and gave her the textbook answer. "The United State Constitution affords each and every citizen the right to due process—which means having competent legal counsel. If all attorneys only defended the innocent, or the non-assholes as you say, our legal system would collapse."

Margo studied me for a moment. She rubbed her chin. "So, you represent assholes because our founding fathers created a system of checks and balances, then?"

I gave a curt nod. "Exactly."

"You want to know what I think?"

Uh. From her tone I wasn't sure I wanted to... Yet, once again, I found myself speaking out of turn.

"Sure."

She stepped closer to me and pushed up on her tippy toes so we were almost nose-to-nose. "I think you're full of shit."

We stared off at each other for a solid thirty seconds, then I couldn't help myself. Unable to keep it in any longer, I cracked. A smile broke out on my face. Then one spread across hers. Next thing I knew, we were both hysterically laughing. Margo held onto her stomach and, at one point, she snorted, which threw us into another round of hysterics.

She wiped tears from her eyes. "Seriously...how do you do it? And don't give me some bullshit answer this time."

I shrugged. "Haven't you ever had a client you didn't care for?"

"Sure. But that's different. I'm only throwing an asshole's parties or planning some elaborate proposal to make them look good. Not beating up my client's adversary who doesn't deserve it."

She had a point. And the truth of the matter was, I was tired of taking on clients with no morals. It was one of the reasons I'd been kicking around leaving my firm and going out on my own. Sometimes you meet with a prospective client and you agree to take on a case, thinking you're representing the kid getting bullied. But after you listen to the other side of the story, you wonder if your client might actually *be* the bully. Those situations, you can't help. But that wasn't what had happened when I met with Rex. My gut had told me he wasn't the victim in the first thirty seconds of sitting down with him. Though it didn't matter, because I was trained to see all clients the same way at my firm—as billable hours.

I sighed. "It's not always the easiest job."

Margo tilted her head and studied me. "Such a shame," she said with a sigh.

"What? That I'm a lawyer?"

"Nope. That you're *Rex's* lawyer."

"Why is that?"

She looked down at her watch and back up to me biting her bottom lip. "Because I'm almost done for the night. And you're standing right under one of the mistletoe I hung this morning."

I looked up. *Holy shit.* I really was. There was nothing more I wanted to do at this moment than take Margo in my arms and kiss the shit out of her. That first kiss had stuck with me for days. But...I couldn't. I was just about to begrudgingly tell her that, when she suddenly turned and started to walk away.

What the...

Margo looked back over her shoulder and flashed the wickedest grin. "Bye-Bye, Mr. Lawyerman. Feel free to watch me walk away now. Unless, of course, that's against the rules, too."

I watched as Margo Adams strutted across the room. Her red dress hugged the curve of her amazing ass as it sashayed from side to side. Honestly, it probably was unethical to drool while checking out your client's adversary, but at this point—I was lucky that was all I allowed myself.

Putting my hands on Margo Adams would totally be a breach of ethics.

Yet in the pit of my stomach, I somehow knew she'd totally be worth it.

CHAPTER 4

Chet

I decided to play a little chicken.

Remember that game? Two drivers careening down the road on the path for a head-on collision. One had to jump out of the way to avoid being run over, which one was generally decided by who had the biggest balls.

"Mr. Saint?" My assistant Lydia buzzed into my office. "Your three o'clock appointment is here."

"Great. Give me five minutes and then show him in."

I cleared the scattered papers of another client's file from my desk and pulled a manila folder from my drawer—my own personal bank statements. Today, I'd definitely have the biggest balls in the room. Though sometimes, on rare occasions, neither party swerved, and a collision just became unavoidable. I thumbed through the folder and turned a few of the top pages over so that the name on the account wasn't visible.

Lydia knocked and opened my door right on time. I stood and buttoned my jacket before coming around my desk.

Rex Adams strolled into my office like he owned the place.

Was he always such an arrogant fuck?

I flashed a practiced, very insincere smile and offered my hand. "Rex. Good to see you. I'm glad you could make it today."

He grumbled. "Three o'clock on a damn Friday. Traffic is terrible."

"Sorry. That's all I had available." Well, except for this morning at ten, and yesterday at eleven, twelve, or one o'clock, and the day before at, well, practically anytime. It was almost Christmas; it wasn't like clients were beating down the door to meet with their divorce attorney. But, I guess I must've forgotten to mention those other available times when I'd called Rex and told him we had to get together before our court appearance next week. *Ooops*. My bad. Sue me.

"Please, have a seat." I motioned to the guest chairs and then lifted a leg to sit on the corner of my desk casually. Position meant a lot during a negotiation. It wasn't a coincidence that I was looking down my nose at Mr. Adams this afternoon. After straightening my tie, I picked up the file with my bank statements from my desk and held it in my hand.

"While we were running a search of possible undisclosed accounts in your wife's name, our team came across another account. This information just recently came to me." I held one side of the folder tight and fanned it so he couldn't read the contents, but could see enough to know that bank statements were inside.

"My wife had another account? I knew that bitch was hiding something."

My jaw flexed. "No, this was an account in your name."

"What account?"

"Well, I suppose it's the one you hadn't told me about." I crossed my arms and readied myself for what might be the biggest bluff of my career. One that could backfire right in my damn face. "It looks like it was funded from withdrawals transferred from a mutual fund of some sort."

Rex didn't seem the slightest bit surprised. "Oh. *That*. The Banco Popular account. That's not in my name. It's in Maribel's name. I'm just the beneficiary."

My brows drew together. "I'm sorry. Who's Maribel?"

"My girl."

"Oh. I see. So this is a new account opened after you moved out of the marital home, then?"

"No. We opened it about two years ago. But like I said, it's not in my name."

What a piece of shit.

I tucked the folder behind me on the desk and folded my hands—mostly to keep from punching this asshole. "We failed to list it on your asset disclosure list that we prepared to file next week," I said matter of factly.

"I'm a beneficiary of a foreign bank account. We don't have to list it."

I had to stifle my laugh. "That's not how it works. We're required to list all *contingent* assets, as well as current assets."

He shifted in his seat. "Just pretend you didn't see it, then."

That's exactly the request I'd been banking on this douche making. "I'm sorry. I can't do that."

"Why not?" Rex's face turned pink from anger.

"Because that would be subordinating fraudulent conduct. It's a violation of ethics."

He jumped up out of his seat and leaned toward me. "But you're a goddamned lawyer!"

I stood. And my six foot two stood a hell of a lot taller than his five foot eight, or whatever the hell he was. "Are you implying that lawyers are unethical?"

He backed up his aggression a bit. "Look. You can't mention that account."

I walked around my desk and sat in my chair. My job was done. Now it was just a matter of whether I fired him or he fired me. It didn't matter to me one way or the other.

I leaned back into my chair feeling a hell of a lot more relaxed. Though Rex was now sitting on the edge of his looking anxious.

"My hands are tied here. Since I know about the account, I can't submit your asset list to the judge and suborn fraud on the court."

"That's bullshit! Your job is to protect my interests."

I held up my hands. "I'm sorry. Either you add the account to your schedule of assets before submitting it to the court, or I won't be able to submit it for you."

"Then, you're fired."

Bingo!

Merry freaking Christmas to me.

There was just one more small thing I needed to do before I left for the holidays. I'd already prepped a Motion to Withdraw as Rex Adam's counsel and handed it off to my paralegal to get filed. After signing into my bank to make sure that my year-end bonus check had cleared, I decided that since giving myself gifts was so much fun, I was going to give myself one more. Taking a stroll down the senior partner hallway, I knocked on the door of the only one in this week—Milton Fleming. I wasn't a fan of his. The few times I'd been invited to executive outings—usually because I had the best golf handicap in the firm—all he did was talk shit about the other associates and which paralegals he'd like to bend over the copy machine.

"Chester. Come on in. How's the golf game going these days?"

Well, it's December in New York, so the courses were pretty much frozen and covered in snow. But I'd play along anyway. "Great. Just great."

"How can I help you?"

I walked to his desk and extended an envelope to him. He reached out and took it.

"I'm giving you my resignation. I've really enjoyed the last five years here at Fleming, O'Shea and Leads, but it's time for me to move on."

His big, bushy brows dipped inward and met in the middle. I never noticed before, but they looked like two fuzzy caterpillars trying to mate. "Is this a matter of money? Were you not happy with your year-end bonus?"

"No, the bonus was fine. Thank you. I appreciate it. I'm just ready to go out on my own."

"Have you already informed your clients?" It was common practice for lawyers to tell their clients before their firm to try to sway them to leave with them when they left.

I shook my head. "Nope. They're all yours."

"This is rather sudden. I thought you were happy here."

I almost laughed at that. How the hell would he know if I was happy? It's not like he'd ever asked. "It's nothing personal." I pointed to the envelope. "I wrote I'd stay on through year end. But I'm flexible if you want me to stay on a little longer."

Milton sighed. "Alright. I'll let the other's know. I'm sure they'll be disappointed to hear the news."

"Have a good holiday," I said.

"Yeah, you, too."

With all of my Christmas gifting done at work, I still had one more little plan I needed to set into motion. I locked up my office and headed for the front door while Googling *Star Events*.

CHAPTER 5

Margo

"Are you up for a little dare?"

God, I was definitely not in the mood. Yet...I couldn't break that stupid streak. I sighed. "Go easy on me. I'm going to have no gifts from Santa under the tree this year, and I'm still pouting over the loss of an elf."

"So I take that as a yes, then?" Nancy raised a brow.

"Yeah. Of course. But be kind. We have to be in court in an hour, and I don't want to be all flustered." Nancy and I met at a coffee shop around the corner from the courthouse. People were walking in and out, and I couldn't help but glance up every time the Christmas bells hanging on the entrance door jingled. My hopes deflated every time it wasn't a certain lawyer. What the hell was wrong with me? Of all the men to become obsessive about, it had to be the one guy I should have zero interest in...and the one guy who wasn't allowed to have any interest in me. I sipped my Peppermint hot chocolate and sighed. "So what's my dare?"

"You see that Salvation Army stand outside?"

I turned to look out the window. "Yeah."

"I just watched Santa leave in a dented Lexus parked in a handicapped spot, even though he seemed perfectly fine to me. Go take that annoying bell off the door and stand outside and sing 'Jingle Bells' until you get someone to stick money in the donation box."

While embarrassing since I couldn't sing for shit, it could have been way worse of a dare with Nancy. I dug my gloves out of my pocket and put them on, then shrugged on my coat before she changed her mind. I wagged a finger at her. "No videoing me."

She raised her hands like she was Little Miss Innocent. "Who me? Never."

I rolled my eyes, but headed for the door. Looking back over my shoulder, no one seemed to be paying attention, so I slipped the bells off the doorknob before going outside and getting into position next to the Salvation Army stand.

"Jingle Bells. Jingle Bells. Jingle All the Way."

Shit. What the hell were the rest of the words? *Eh. Who cares.* I turned around to make sure my friend saw me and started to sing the only verse I apparently knew a second time while waving to her.

"Jingle Bells. Jingle Bells. Jingle All the Way."

Nancy lifted her hands, palms up and motioned up and down, indicating that I should sing louder. So I did while smiling like an idiot at her.

"Jingle Bells!"

"Jingle Bells!"

"Jingle All the Way!"

Nancy gave me a thumbs up, and I continued my screaming rendition of the eight-word chorus of "Jingle Bells" as I turned around...only to find a man standing right in front of me.

And not just any man.

Chet.

"Jingle Be—" I froze.

He arched a brow. "Second job?"

"It's a dare. Can you just shove a dollar in the pot so I can stop?"

Chet dug his wallet out of the front pocket of his slacks and slipped a ten-dollar bill from the fold. He waved it in front of me. "So all I need to do is drop this in the bucket, and you can stop singing?"

"Yes."

He grinned from ear to ear, then tucked the cash back in his pocket and folded his arms. Taking a few steps back, he leaned against a column. "Keep singing."

My jaw dropped. "Are you joking? You're really not going to help me?"

"Not until after I enjoy a little of the show."

I squinted at him.

The jerk squinted back with a smirk.

A nice looking elderly couple started to walk toward the coffee shop door. So I stuck my tongue out at Chet and started to sing in their direction.

"Jingle Bells! Jingle Bells! Jingle All the Way!"

The couple turned their heads and walked right past to go inside.

Chet started to belly laugh.

This went on for a solid five minutes. At least a half-a-dozen people passed by, all of whom ignored me. Finally, Nancy walked out. She put a five into the donation bin and handed me my hot chocolate while laughing. "The dogs in the neighborhood are howling. I had to put them out of their misery. Plus, it's time to go to court."

Chet nodded. "Thanks for the show, ladies. I'll see you in court."

"Your Honor, I have a motion to file today."

The impatient Judge Halloran made a face and motioned with his hand for Chet to approach the bench.

I leaned to Nancy and whispered, "What's going on?"

She shook her head. "No idea. First I'm hearing about it."

Chet handed some papers to the judge and then walked to our table and handed a similar packet to Nancy. "Sorry about the last-minute service," he said. Then the bastard had the balls to wink at me. *He winked at me!*

My attorney and the judge flipped through the pages while I waited for someone to tell me what the hell was going on now.

Judge Halloran took off his glasses and rubbed his eyes. "Mr. Adams, please stand."

My almost ex-husband stood at the table across from us.

"Your attorney has filed a Motion to Withdraw, stating that you've terminated his services. Is this correct?"

What? My eyes widened, and my head whipped to Nancy, who shushed me and shook her head.

"Yes, that's correct, Your Honor."

Halloran sighed. "I hate delays. While this is your right, I'm telling you right now that this will be the last continuance granted for the remainder of this case. As long as opposing counsel doesn't object, I'm scheduling this hearing for the first week in January. Have you hired a new attorney?"

"Yes, Your Honor."

"Then where is he today?"

"He's in the Bahamas for vacation. But he's back the day after New Year's."

The judge mumbled. "Of course he is." He looked over at our table. "Ms. Davis, do you object to counsel's withdrawal and a *very* short continuance to allow new counsel to get caught up to speed?"

Nancy shook her head. "No, Your Honor. That's fine with me."

The judge slipped his glasses back onto his face. "Motion to Withdraw granted. Today's hearing is rescheduled for January 5th." He slammed his gavel, and everyone started to pack up their stuff.

"Uh. What just happened?" I said to Nancy.

She smiled. "Merry Christmas. I hope you enjoy my gift."

"I don't understand. You just allowed my divorce to be delayed again and you think that's *a gift*?"

She leaned closer. "It is. Because now that Chet isn't Rex's attorney, you can bang his brains out. Just make sure you wrap that gift up. You're welcome."

I never did hear from Chet after he left the courthouse that day.

After a quiet holiday spent with my family in Queens, I felt rejuvenated. It was unlike me to take a short break from work, but it was long overdue.

I hadn't planned on working until after the New Year, but when I received a call a few days after Christmas requesting me to plan a private dinner that would pay triple my normal rate, I decided to accept it. It was a lot of money for a small event for two, and I knew I could throw it together in no time. It was particularly a no-brainer because the client's assistant told me I could literally do whatever I wanted. Those were the types of assignments I really had a hard time turning down. When I was given free rein, I was like a kid in a candy store. The best part was: even though the party was on New Year's Eve, all of the setup would be completed fairly early. I would only have to show up at the beginning of the dinner to make sure preparations had gone off without a hitch, and I would still be able to salvage most of the evening.

Not that I had any plans aside from watching Ryan Seacrest while inhaling a tub of Ben and Jerry's Cherry Garcia. There would be no hot New Year's Eve date. There would be no kissing anyone at the stroke of midnight. Unfortunately, as much as I hated to admit it, I still found myself too hung up on fantasies of Chet Saint to even want to put myself out there.

I still couldn't believe he was no longer Rex's lawyer, though. A part of my wild imagination had hoped that maybe he'd take advantage of the fact that he was now free from our *conflict of interest* in order to pursue me. But if that were the case, he would've called or texted. So, the fact that I hadn't heard from him proved that we weren't on the same page.

Despite the volatile start, our chemistry had been palpable at that holiday costume party. It was clear that if Rex weren't in the way, we would've continued what we'd started at the café. I did wonder what had caused Rex to fire him. I liked to believe that maybe Chet truly got fed up with the type of person Rex is and stood up to him, refusing to play my ex's games. Now Chet was free of Rex. If only I could say the same.

I'd just arrived at the venue I'd booked for my New Year's Eve event to make sure all of the right accommodations were in place. I'd called all of my contacts at the best hotels overlooking Times Square and was finally able to find a private suite that would allow my client a view of the ball dropping tonight without having to endure the cold and crowds below. It was the best of both worlds. My go-to caterer agreed to put together a last-minute spread of Moroccan cuisine. Why Moroccan? Because I could choose whatever the heck I wanted, and it had been a while since I'd thrown a Moroccan-themed party.

The room looked exactly how I'd asked my assistants to set it up. A traditional Moroccan table runner was draped across a table. Colorful lamps were placed strategically throughout the space. We brought in jewel-toned drapes and satin pillows in various colors. It truly looked mystical with a royal flair. Moroccan Gnawa music would be played from a speaker in a continuous loop, since the client wanted privacy, specifically requesting that they be alone, so that meant no live violinist or any other musician.

The client had requested to meet me before his private party began, so my plan was to stick around long enough to make that introduction. I'd worn a deep purple dress to match the décor. I was looking out the window at the lights below as I awaited the client's arrival. He would apparently be coming earlier than his lady friend to ensure everything met his needs before he surprised her with this dinner. I hadn't spoken with him, only to his assistant. Given that this was an intimate party for two, I wondered if maybe he planned to propose tonight or something.

"Ms. Adams?"

A deep voice startled me as I stared out the window. I turned around, and my smile faded into pure shock. A man was dressed to the nines in a fitted tux. He was also the last man I ever imagined I'd see: Chester Saint.

Chet.

What is he doing here?

He cleared his throat as he looked down at my purple dress. "I hope you can stay."

He looked stunning in that tux. And me? I was just *stunned*. Looking around in shock, I said, "Stay? All of this...it's for me? *You're* my client?"

"I know this was a dramatic way of getting you to go out with me. But I felt like after the rocky way we met, I owed you a proper night out."

My hand was still on my chest as I took a few steps toward him, my legs feeling wobbly. "Actually, the way we technically met is probably one of my best memories."

He smiled. "That's true. The way we met in that café was actually pretty damn nice. *Rocky* referred to everything that happened *after* that day."

The lights from Times Square flashed through the large window. But there was no amount of outside distraction that could take my eyes off him.

"You could've just taken me to Five Guys for burgers, you know," I said. "That would have been good enough."

"I figured by having you plan this private dinner, everything would be perfect and exactly to your liking."

"Here I was thinking that whoever this woman was— she was the luckiest chick on the planet. I never imagined *she* was...*me*."

He smiled, placing his hands in his pockets and looking so incredibly handsome. "Are you okay with this...joining me for dinner?"

That was a no-brainer.

My body filled with excitement as I eagerly nodded. "Yes."

We were just inches apart when he said, "I haven't

been able to stop thinking about you. After our conversation at the holiday party, continuing to represent Rex just felt wrong. For more reasons than one."

"Is it wrong that I was relieved that he fired you?"

His mouth curved into a smile. "Let's just say I might have set myself up for it." He winked.

I knew it. He *wanted* to be fired.

"Did your firm give you trouble about it?"

"No. In fact, I quit the firm that same day. I'm starting my own practice and honestly couldn't be happier."

What?

It thrilled me to hear that. I would've hated for him to have hurt his career because of what happened with my loser ex.

"Chet, that's amazing. Truly. A fresh start."

He paused before he said, "I want that with you, too—a fresh start. I'd really like to take up where we left off that day in the café."

Shivers ran down my spine. There was nothing more I'd wanted. "I'd like that."

He looked down at my dress, then back up at me. "You look like a dream. So beautiful."

"So do you." Nervously giggling, I shook my head. "I mean, handsome."

"Well, the last time you saw me dressed up, I was Buddy the Elf, so anything is an improvement." He winked.

Over the next few hours, we sat down and enjoyed the spicy delicacies that my caterer had made. Instead of sitting at the table, we lounged comfortably on some satin pillows on the floor while the Moroccan music played on low volume in the background. It was truly magical.

Chet listened intently as I told him the full story about Rex's and my marriage. He also told me about some of his past relationships. We talked about our careers and our hopes and dreams for the future. We opened up to each other about a lot of things, and it was one of the best conversations I'd had in a very long time. It was long overdue.

At a certain point, we were looking into each other's eyes, and I could feel his desire in my bones when he said, "I told myself I was going to wait until midnight to kiss you, but I really want to do it right now."

Without overthinking it, I answered him, silently, by leaning in and placing my lips over his. He groaned into my mouth as I fell into him.

His mouth was hot and so hungry for me. The feeling of euphoria that I remembered from that day in the café was instantly familiar, except this time it was amplified by the sensation of his hard body pressed against me. It had felt like forever since I'd been with a man, and I realized that I wanted Chet more than I'd wanted anything in a very long time.

Raking my hands through his silky hair, I pulled him closer as our kiss grew deeper. With every second that passed, we became more lost in each other. I could feel his hot erection through the material of his pants. *I wanted him.*

When I'd kissed him that first day in the café, it was because I was *trying* to prove my impulsivity. There was no need to *try* tonight. I couldn't stop where this was going, even if I'd wanted to. It had never felt so natural to let loose and let myself get lost in someone. And thankfully, despite what his last name might imply—Chester was no *saint*. And that was fine by me.

Needless to say, we never did get to watch the ball drop. But it didn't matter, because the fireworks inside our suite were bigger than anything happening outside in Times Square. And somehow, I knew that this year was

THE END

Happy Holidays to all of our readers!
We dare you to do something
impulsive and fun in 2020!

STALK US, WE LIKE IT!

Facebook Fan Groups
Penelope: https://www.facebook.com/groups/
PenelopesPeeps/

Vi: https://www.facebook.com/groups/
ViKeelandFanGroup/

Instagram
Penelope: https://instagram/PenelopeWardAuthor

Vi: https://www.instagram.com/vi_keeland/

Websites
Penelope: www.penelopewardauthor.com

Vi: www.vikeeland.com

OTHER BOOKS BY
PENELOPE WARD & VI KEELAND

Hate Notes

Park Avenue Player

British Bedmate

Mister Moneybags

Playboy Pilot

Stuck-Up Suit

Cocky Bastard

The Rush Series

Rebel Heir

Rebel Heart

ABOUT PENELOPE WARD

Penelope Ward is a *New York Times, USA Today* and *#1 Wall Street Journal* bestselling author.

She grew up in Boston with five older brothers and spent most of her twenties as a television news anchor. Penelope resides in Rhode Island with her husband, son and beautiful daughter with autism.

With over 1.5 million books sold, she is a twenty-time *New York Times* bestseller and the author of over twenty novels.

Penelope's books have been translated into over a dozen languages and can be found in bookstores around the world.

Subscribe to Penelope's newsletter here:
http://bit.ly/1X725rj

OTHER BOOKS BY PENELOPE WARD

The Day He Came Back
When August Ends
Love Online
Gentleman Nine
Drunk Dial
Mack Daddy
RoomHate
Stepbrother Dearest
Neighbor Dearest
Jaded and Tyed (A novelette)
Sins of Sevin
Jake Undone (Jake #1)
Jake Understood (Jake #2)
My Skylar
Gemini

ABOUT VI KEELAND

Vi Keeland is a #1 *New York Times*, #1 *Wall Street Journal*, and *USA Today* Bestselling author. With millions of books sold, her titles have appeared in over a hundred Bestseller lists and are currently translated in twenty-five languages. She resides in New York with her husband and their three children where she is living out her own happily ever after with the boy she met at age six.

OTHER BOOKS BY VI KEELAND

All Grown Up
We Shouldn't
The Naked Truth
Sex, Not Love
Beautiful Mistake
EgoManiac
Bossman
The Baller
Left Behind (A Young Adult Novel)
First Thing I See

Life on Stage series (2 standalone books)
Beat
Throb

MMA Fighter series (3 standalone books)
Worth the Fight
Worth the Chance
Worth Forgiving

The Cole Series (2 book serial)
Belong to You
Made for You